Something of Myself: For My Friends Known and Unknown

Rudyard Kipling

CONTENTS

Chapter I

A Very Young Person

1865-1878

Give me the first six years of a child's life and you can have the rest.

Looking back from this my seventieth year, it seems to me that every card in my working life has been dealt me in such a manner that I had but to play it as it came. Therefore, ascribing all good fortune to Allah the Dispenser of Events, I begin: —

My first impression is of daybreak, light and colour and golden and purple fruits at the level of my shoulder. This would be the memory of early morning walks to the Bombay fruit market with my ayah and later with my sister in her perambulator, and of our returns with our purchases piled high on the bows of it. Our ayah was a Portuguese Roman Catholic who would pray—I beside her—at a wayside Cross. Meeta, my Hindu bearer, would sometimes go into little Hindu temples where, being below the age of caste, I held his hand and looked at the dimly-seen, friendly Gods.

Our evening walks were by the sea in the shadow of palm-groves which, I think, were called the Mahim Woods. When the wind blew the great nuts would tumble, and we fled—my ayah, and my sister in her perambulator—to the safety of the open. I have always felt the menacing darkness of tropical eventides, as I have loved the voices of night-winds through palm or banana leaves, and the song of the tree-frogs.

There were far-going Arab dhows on the pearly waters, and gaily dressed Parsees wading out to worship the sunset. Of their creed I knew nothing, nor did I know that near our little house on the Bombay Esplanade were the Towers of Silence, where their Dead are exposed to the waiting vultures on the rim of the towers, who scuffle and spread wings when they see the bearers of the Dead below. I did not understand my Mother's distress when she found 'a child's hand' in our garden, and said I was not to ask questions about it. I wanted to see that child's hand. But my ayah told me.

In the afternoon heats before we took our sleep, she or Meeta would tell us stories and Indian nursery songs all unforgotten, and we were sent into the dining-room after we had been dressed, with the caution 'Speak English now to Papa and Mamma. ' So one spoke 'English, ' haltingly translated out of the vernacular idiom that one thought and dreamed in. The Mother sang wonderful songs at a black piano and would go out to Big Dinners. Once she came back, very quickly, and told me, still awake, that 'the big Lord Sahib' had been killed and there was to be no Big Dinner. This was Lord Mayo, assassinated by a native. Meeta explained afterwards that he had been 'hit with a knife. ' Meeta unconsciously saved me from any night terrors or dread of the dark. Our ayah, with a servant's curious mixture of deep affection and shallow device, had told me that a stuffed leopard's head on the nursery wall was there to see that I went to sleep. But Meeta spoke of it scornfully as 'the head of an animal, ' and I took it off my mind as a fetish, good or bad, for it was only some unspecified 'animal. '

Far across green spaces round the house was a marvellous place filled with smells of paints and oils, and lumps of clay with which I played. That was the atelier of my Father's School of Art, and a Mr. 'Terry Sahib' his assistant, to whom my small sister was devoted, was our great friend. Once, on the way there alone, I passed the edge of a huge ravine a foot deep, where a winged monster as big as myself attacked me, and I fled and wept. My Father drew for me a picture of the tragedy with a rhyme beneath: —

There was a small boy in Bombay
Who once from a hen ran away.
    When they said: 'You're a baby,
    ' He replied: 'Well, I may be:
But I don't like these hens of Bombay. '

This consoled me. I have thought well of hens ever since.

Then those days of strong light and darkness passed, and there was a time in a ship with an immense semi-circle blocking all vision on each side of her. (She must have been the old paddlewheel P. &O. Ripon.) There was a train across a desert (the Suez Canal was not yet opened) and a halt in it, and a small girl wrapped in a shawl on the seat opposite me, whose face stands out still. There was next a dark land, and a darker room full of cold, in one wall of which a white woman made naked fire, and I cried aloud with dread, for I had never before seen a grate.

Then came a new small house smelling of aridity and emptiness, and a parting in the dawn with Father and Mother, who said that I must learn quickly to read and write so that they might send me letters and books.

I lived in that house for close on six years. It belonged to a woman who took in children whose parents were in India. She was married to an old Navy Captain, who had been a midshipman at Navarino, and had afterwards been entangled in a harpoon-line while whale-fishing, and dragged down till he miraculously freed himself. But the line had scarred his ankle for life—a dry, black scar, which I used to look at with horrified interest.

The house itself stood in the extreme suburbs of Southsea, next to a Portsmouth unchanged in most particulars since Trafalgar—the Portsmouth of Sir Walter Besant's By Celia's Arbour. The timber for a Navy that was only experimenting with iron-clads such as the Inflexible lay in great booms in the Harbour. The little training-brigs kept their walks opposite Southsea Castle, and Portsmouth Hard was as it had always been. Outside these things lay the desolation of Hayling Island, Lumps Fort, and the isolated hamlet of Milton. I would go for long walks with the Captain, and once he took me to see a ship called the Alert (or Discovery) returned from Arctic explorations, her decks filled with old sledges and lumber, and her spare rudder being cut up for souvenirs. A sailor gave me a piece, but I lost it. Then the old Captain died, and I was sorry, for he was the only person in that house as far as I can remember who ever threw me a kind word.

It was an establishment run with the full vigour of the Evangelical as revealed to the Woman. I had never heard of Hell, so I was introduced to it in all its terrors—I and whatever luckless little slavey might be in the house, whom severe rationing had led to steal food. Once I saw the Woman beat such a girl who picked up the kitchen poker and threatened retaliation. Myself I was regularly beaten. The Woman had an only son of twelve or thirteen as religious as she. I was a real joy to him, for when his mother had finished with me for the day he (we slept in the same room) took me on and roasted the other side.

If you cross-examine a child of seven or eight on his day's doings (specially when he wants to go to sleep) he will contradict himself very satisfactorily. If each contradiction be set down as a lie and retailed at breakfast, life is not easy. I have known a certain amount of bullying, but this was calculated torture—religious as well as scientific. Yet it made me give attention to the lies I soon found it necessary to tell: and this, I presume, is the foundation of literary effort.

But my ignorance was my salvation. I was made to read without explanation, under the usual fear of punishment. And on a day that I remember it came to me that 'reading' was not 'the Cat lay on the Mat, ' but a means to everything that would make me happy. So I read all that came within my reach. As soon as my pleasure in this was known, deprivation from reading was added to my punishments. I then read by stealth and the more earnestly.

There were not many books in that house, but Father and Mother as soon as they heard I could read sent me priceless volumes. One I have still, a bound copy of Aunt Judy's Magazine of the early 'seventies, in which appeared Mrs. Ewing's Six to Sixteen. I owe more in circuitous ways to that tale than I can tell. I knew it, as I know it still, almost by heart. Here was a history of real people and real things. It was better than Knatchbull-Hugessen's Tales at Tea-time, better even than The Old Shikarri with its steel engravings of charging pigs and angry tigers. On another plane was an old magazine with Scott's 'I climbed the dark brow of the mighty

4

Helvellyn. ' I knew nothing of its meaning but the words moved and pleased. So did other extracts from the poems of 'A. Tennyson. '

A visitor, too, gave me a little purple book of severely moral tendency called The Hope of the Katzekopfs—about a bad boy made virtuous, but it contained verses that began, 'Farewell Rewards and Fairies, ' and ended with an injunction 'To pray for the "noddle" of William Churne of Staffordshire. ' This bore fruit afterwards.

And somehow or other I came across a tale about a lion-hunter in South Africa who fell among lions who were all Freemasons, and with them entered into a confederacy against some wicked baboons. I think that, too, lay dormant until the Jungle Books began to be born.

There comes to my mind here a memory of two books of verse about child-life which I have tried in vain to identify. One—blue and fat— described 'nine white wolves' coming 'over the wold' and stirred me to the deeps; and also certain savages who 'thought the name of England was something that could not burn. '

The other book—brown and fat—was full of lovely tales in strange metres. A girl was turned into a water-rat 'as a matter of course'; an Urchin cured an old man of gout by means of a cool cabbage-leaf, and somehow 'forty wicked Goblins' were mixed up in the plot; and a 'Darling' got out on the house-leads with a broom and tried to sweep stars off the skies. It must have been an unusual book for that age, but I have never been able to recover it, any more than I have a song that a nursemaid sang at low-tide in the face of the sunset on Littlehampton Sands when I was less than six. But the impression of wonder, excitement and terror and the red bars of failing light is as clear as ever.

Among the servants in the House of Desolation was one from Cumnor, which name I associated with sorrow and darkness and a raven that 'flapped its wings. ' Years later I identified the lines: 'And thrice the Raven flapped her wing Around the towers of Cumnor Hall. ' But how and where I first heard the lines that cast the shadow is beyond me—unless it be that the brain holds everything that passes within reach of the senses, and it is only ourselves who do not know this.

When my Father sent me a Robinson Crusoe with steel engravings I set up in business alone as a trader with savages (the wreck parts of the tale never much interested me), in a mildewy basement room where I stood my solitary confinements. My apparatus was a coconut shell strung on a red cord, a tin trunk, and a piece of packing-case which kept off any other world. Thus fenced about, everything inside the fence was quite real, but mixed with the smell of damp cupboards. If the bit of board fell, I had to begin the magic all over again. I have learned since from children who play much alone that this rule of 'beginning again in a pretend game' is not uncommon. The magic, you see, lies in the ring or fence that you take refuge in.

Once I remember being taken to a town called Oxford and a street called Holywell, where I was shown an Ancient of Days who, I was told, was the Provost of Oriel; wherefore I never understood, but conceived him to be some sort of idol. And twice or thrice we went, all of us, to pay a day-long visit to an old gentleman in a house in the country near Havant. Here everything was wonderful and unlike my world, and he had an old lady sister who was kind, and I played in hot, sweet-smelling meadows and ate all sorts of things.

After such a visit I was once put through the third degree by the Woman and her son, who asked me if I had told the old gentleman that I was much fonder of him than was the Woman's son. It must have been the tail-end of some sordid intrigue or other—the old gentleman being of kin to that unhappy pair—but it was beyond my comprehension. My sole concern had been a friendly pony in the paddock. My dazed attempts to clear myself were not accepted and, once again, the pleasure that I was seen to have taken was balanced by punishments and humiliation—above all humiliation. That alternation was quite regular. I can but admire the infernal laborious ingenuity of it all. Exempli gratia. Coming out of church once I smiled. The Devil-Boy demanded why. I said I didn't know, which was child's truth. He replied that I must know. People didn't laugh for nothing. Heaven knows what explanation I put forward; but it was duly reported to the Woman as a 'lie.' Result, afternoon upstairs with the Collect to learn. I learned most of the Collects that way and a great deal of the Bible. The son after three or four years went into a Bank and was generally too tired on his return to torture me, unless things had gone wrong with him. I learned to know what was coming from his step into the house.

But, for a month each year I possessed a paradise which I verily believe saved me. Each December I stayed with my Aunt Georgie, my mother's sister, wife of Sir Edward Burne-Jones, at The Grange, North End Road. At first I must have been escorted there, but later I went alone, and arriving at the house would reach up to the open-work iron bell-pull on the wonderful gate that let me into all felicity. When I had a house of my own, and The Grange was emptied of meaning, I begged for and was given that bell-pull for my entrance, in the hope that other children might also feel happy when they rang it.

At The Grange I had love and affection as much as the greediest, and I was not very greedy, could desire. There were most wonderful smells of paints and turpentine whiffing down from the big studio on the first floor where my Uncle worked; there was the society of my two cousins, and a sloping mulberry tree which we used to climb for our plots and conferences. There was a rocking-horse in the nursery and a table that, tilted up on two chairs, made a toboggan-slide of the best. There were pictures finished or half finished of lovely colours; and in the rooms chairs and cupboards such as the world had not yet seen, for William Morris (our Deputy 'Uncle Topsy') was just beginning to fabricate these things. There was an incessant come and go of young people and grown-ups all willing to play with us—except an elderly person called 'Browning,' who took no proper interest in the skirmishes which happened to be raging on his entry. Best of all, immeasurably, was the beloved Aunt herself reading us The Pirate or The Arabian Nights of evenings, when one lay out on the big sofas sucking toffee, and calling our cousins 'Ho, Son,' or 'Daughter of my Uncle' or 'True Believer.'

Often the Uncle, who had a 'golden voice, ' would assist in our evening play, though mostly he worked at black and white in the middle of our riots. He was never idle. We made a draped chair in the hall serve for the seat of 'Norna of the Fitful Head' and addressed her questions till the Uncle got inside the rugs and gave us answers which thrilled us with delightful shivers, in a voice deeper than all the boots in the world. And once he descended in broad daylight with a tube of 'Mummy Brown' in his hand, saying that he had discovered it was made of dead Pharaohs and we must bury it accordingly. So we all went out and helped—according to the rites of Mizraim and Memphis, I hope—and—to this day I could drive a spade within a foot of where that tube lies.

At bedtime one hastened along the passages, where unfinished cartoons lay against the walls. The Uncle often painted in their eyes first, leaving the rest in charcoal—a most effective presentation. Hence our speed to our own top-landing, where we could hang over the stairs and listen to the loveliest sound in the world—deep-voiced men laughing together over dinner.

It was a jumble of delights and emotions culminating in being allowed to blow the big organ in the studio for the beloved Aunt, while the Uncle worked, or 'Uncle Topsy' came in full of some business of picture-frames or stained glass or general denunciations. Then it was hard to keep the little lead weight on its string below the chalk mark, and if the organ ran out in squeals the beloved Aunt would be sorry. Never, never angry!

As a rule Morris took no notice of anything outside what was in his mind at the moment. But I remember one amazing exception. My cousin Margaret and I, then about eight, were in the nursery eating pork-dripping on brown bread, which is a dish for the Gods, when we heard 'Uncle Topsy' in the hall calling, as he usually did, for 'Ned' or 'Georgie. ' The matter was outside our world. So we were the more impressed when, not finding the grown-ups, he came in and said he would tell us a story. We settled ourselves under the table which we used for a toboggan-slide and he, gravely as ever, climbed on to our big rocking-horse. There, slowly surging back and forth while the poor beast creaked, he told us a tale full of fascinating horrors, about a man who was condemned to dream bad dreams. One of them took the shape of a cow's tail waving from a heap of dried fish. He went away as abruptly as he had come. Long afterwards, when I was old enough to know a maker's pains, it dawned on me that we must have heard the Saga of Burnt Njal, which was then interesting him. In default of grown-ups, and pressed by need to pass the story between his teeth and clarify it, he had used us.

But on a certain day—one tried to fend off the thought of it—the delicious dream would end, and one would return to the House of Desolation, and for the next two or three mornings there cry on waking up. Hence more punishments and cross-examinations.

Often and often afterwards, the beloved Aunt would ask me why I had never told any one how I was being treated. Children tell little more than animals, for what comes to them they accept as eternally established. Also, badly-treated children have a clear notion of what they are likely to get if they betray the secrets of a prison-house before they are clear of it.

In justice to the Woman I can say that I was adequately fed. (I remember a gift to her of some red 'fruit' called 'tomatoes' which, after long consideration, she boiled with sugar; and they were very beastly. The tinned meat of those days was Australian beef with a crumbly fat, and string-boiled mutton, hard to get down.) Nor was my life an unsuitable preparation for my future, in that it demanded constant wariness, the habit of observation, and attendance on moods and tempers; the noting of discrepancies between speech and action; a certain reserve of demeanour; and automatic suspicion of sudden favours. Brother Lippo Lippi, in his own harder case, as a boy discovered: —

Why, soul and sense of him grow sharp alike,
He learns the look of things, and none the less
For admonition.

So it was with me.

My troubles settled themselves in a few years. My eyes went wrong, and I could not well see to read. For which reason I read the more and in bad lights. My work at the terrible little dayschool where I had been sent suffered in consequence, and my monthly reports showed it. The loss of 'reading-time' was the worst of my 'home' punishments for bad school-work. One report was so bad that I threw it away and said that I had never received it. But this is a hard world for the amateur liar. My web of deceit was swiftly exposed—the Son spared time after banking-hours to help in the auto-da-fé—and I was well beaten and sent to school through the streets of Southsea with the placard 'Liar' between my shoulders. In the long run these things, and many more of the like, drained me of any capacity for real, personal hate for the rest of my days. So close must any life-filling passion lie to its opposite. 'Who having known the Diamond will concern himself with glass? '

Some sort of nervous breakdown followed, for I imagined I saw shadows and things that were not there, and they worried me more than the Woman. The beloved Aunt must have heard of it, and a man came down to see me as to my eyes and reported that I was half-blind. This, too, was supposed to be 'showing-off, ' and I was segregated from my sister—another punishment—as a sort of moral leper. Then—I do not remember that I had any warning—the Mother returned from India. She told me afterwards that when she first came up to my room to kiss me goodnight, I flung up an arm to guard off the cuff that I had been trained to expect.

I was taken at once from the House of Desolation, and for months ran wild in a little farm-house on the edge of Epping Forest, where I was not encouraged to refer to my guilty past. Except for my spectacles, which were uncommon in those days, I was completely happy with my Mother and the local society, which included for me a gipsy of the name of Saville, who told me tales of selling horses to the ignorant; the farmer's wife; her niece Patty who turned a kind blind eye on our raids into the dairy; the postman; and the farm-boys. The farmer did not approve of my teaching one of his cows to stand and be milked in the field. My Mother drew the line at my return to meals red-booted from assisting at the slaughter of swine, or reeking after the exploration of attractive muck heaps. These were the only restrictions I recall.

A cousin, afterwards to be a Prime Minister, would come down on visits. The farmer said that we did each other 'no good. ' Yet the worst I can remember was our self-sacrificing war against a wasps' nest on a muddy islet in a most muddy pond. Our only weapons were switches of broom, but we defeated the enemy unscathed. The trouble at home centred round an enormous currant roly-poly—a 'spotted dog' afoot long. We took it away to sustain us in action and we heard a great deal about it from Patty in the evening.

Then we went to London and stayed for some weeks in a tiny lodging-house in the semi-rural Brompton Road, kept by an ivory-faced, lordly-whiskered ex-butler and his patient wife. Here, for the first time, it happened that the night got into my head. I rose up and wandered about that still house till daybreak, when I slipped out into the little brick-walled garden and saw the dawn break. All would have been well but for Pluto, a pet toad brought back from Epping Forest, who lived mostly in one of my pockets. It struck me that he might be thirsty, and I stole into my Mother's room and would have given him drink from a water jug. But it slipped and broke and very much was said. The ex-butler could not understand why I had stayed awake all night. I did not know then that such nightwakings would be laid upon me through my life; or that my fortunate hour would be on the turn of sunrise, with a sou'-west breeze afoot.

The sorely tried Mother got my sister and me season-tickets for the old South Kensington Museum which was only across the road. (No need in those days to caution us against the traffic.) Very shortly we two, on account of our regular attendance (for the weather had turned wet), owned that place and one policeman in special. When we came with any grown-ups he saluted us magnificently. From the big Buddha with the little door in his back, to the towering dull-gilt ancient coaches and carven chariots in long dark corridors—even the places marked 'private' where fresh treasures were always being unpacked—we roved at will, and divided the treasures child-fashion. There were instruments of music inlaid with lapis, beryl and ivories; glorious gold-fretted spinets and clavichords; the bowels of the great Glastonbury clock; mechanical models steel- and silver-butted pistols, daggers and arquebusses—the labels alone were an education; a collection of precious stones and rings—we quarrelled over those—and a big bluish book which was the manuscript of one of Dickens' novels. That man seemed to me to have written very carelessly; leaving out lots which he had to squeeze in between the lines afterwards.

These experiences were a soaking in colour and design with, above all, the proper Museum smell; and it stayed with me. By the end of that long holiday I understood that my Mother had written verses, that my Father 'wrote things' also; that books and pictures were among the most important affairs in the world; that I could read as much as I chose and ask the meaning of things from any one I met. I had found out, too, that one could take pen and set down what one thought, and that nobody accused one of 'showing off' by so doing. I read a good deal; Sidonia the Sorceress; Emerson's poems; and Bret Harte's stories; and I learned all sorts of verses for the pleasure of repeating them to myself in bed.

Chapter II

The School Before Its Time

1878-1882

Then came school at the far end of England. The Head of it was a lean, slow-spoken, bearded, Arab-complexioned man whom till then I had known as one of my Deputy-Uncles at The Grange—Cormell Price, otherwise 'Uncle Crom. ' My Mother, on her return to India, confided my sister and me to the care of three dear ladies who lived off the far end of Kensington High Street over against Addison Road, in a house filled with books, peace, kindliness, patience and what to-day would be called 'culture. ' But it was natural atmosphere.

One of the ladies wrote novels on her knee, by the fireside, sitting just outside the edge of conversation, beneath two clay pipes tied with black ribbon, which once Carlyle had smoked. All the people one was taken to see either wrote or painted pictures or, as in the case of a Mr. and Miss de Morgan, ornamented tiles. They let me play with their queer, sticky paints. Somewhere in the background were people called Jean Ingelow and Christina Rossetti, but I was never lucky enough to see those good spirits. And there was choice in the walls of bookshelves of anything one liked from Firmilian to The Moonstone and The Woman in White and, somehow, all Wellington's Indian Despatches, which fascinated me.

These treasures were realised by me in the course of the next few years. Meantime (Spring of '78), after my experience at Southsea, the prospect of school did not attract. The United Services College was in the nature of a company promoted by poor officers and the like for the cheap education of their sons, and set up at Westward Ho! near Bideford. It was largely a caste-school—some seventy-five per cent of us had been born outside England and hoped to follow their fathers in the Army. It was but four or five years old when I joined, and had been made up under Cormell Price's hand by drafts from Haileybury, whose pattern it followed, and, I think, a percentage of 'hard cases' from other schools. Even by the standards of those days, it was primitive in its appointments, and our food would now raise a mutiny in Dartmoor. I remember no time, after home tips had been spent, when we would not eat dry bread if we could steal it from the trays in the basement before tea. Yet the sick-house was permanently empty except for lawful accidents; I remember not one death of a boy; and only one epidemic—of chicken-pox. Then the Head called us together and condoled with us in such fashion that we expected immediate break-up and began to cheer. But he said that, perhaps, the best thing would be to take no notice of the incident, and that he would 'work us lightly' for the rest of the term. He did and it checked the epidemic.

Naturally, Westward Ho! was brutal enough, but, setting aside the foul speech that a boy ought to learn early and put behind him by his seventeenth year, it was clean with a cleanliness that I have never heard of in any other school. I remember no cases of even suspected perversion, and am inclined to the theory that if masters did not suspect them, and show that they suspected, there would not be quite so many elsewhere. Talking things over with Cormell Price afterwards, he confessed that his one prophylactic against certain unclean microbes was to 'send us to bed dead tired. ' Hence the wideness of our bounds, and his deaf ear towards our incessant riots and wars between the Houses.

At the end of my first term, which was horrible, my parents could not reach England for the Easter holidays, and I had to stay up with a few big boys reading for Army Exams. and a batch of youngsters whose people were very far away. I expected the worst, but when we survivors were left in the echoing form-rooms after the others had driven cheering to the station, life suddenly became a new thing (thanks to Cormell Price). The big remote seniors turned into tolerant elder brothers, and let us small fry rove far out of bounds; shared their delicacies with us at tea; and even took an interest in our hobbies. We had no special work to do and enjoyed ourselves hugely. On the return of the school 'all smiles stopped together, ' which was right and proper. For compensation I was given a holiday when my Father came home, and with him went to the Paris

Exhibition of '78, where he was in charge of Indian Exhibits. He allowed me, at twelve years old, the full freedom of that spacious and friendly city, and the run of the Exhibition grounds and buildings. It was an education in itself; and set my life-long love for France. Also, he saw to it that I should learn to read French at least for my own amusement, and gave me Jules Verne to begin with. French as an accomplishment was not well-seen at English schools in my time, and knowledge of it connoted leanings towards immorality. For myself; —

I hold it truth with him who sung
    Unpublished melodies,
Who wakes in Paris, being young,
    O' summer, wakes in Paradise.

For those who may be still interested in such matters, I wrote of this part of my life in some Souvenirs of France, which are very close to the facts of that time.

My first year and a half was not pleasant. The most persistent bullying comes less from the bigger boys, who merely kick and pass on, than from young devils of fourteen acting in concert against one butt. Luckily for me I was physically some years in advance of my age, and swimming in the big open sea baths, or off the Pebble Ridge, was the one accomplishment that brought me any credit. I played footer (Rugby Union), but here again my sight hampered me. I was not even in the Second Fifteen.

After my strength came suddenly to me about my fourteenth year, there was no more bullying; and either my natural sloth or past experience did not tempt me to bully in my turn. I had by then found me two friends with whom, by a carefully arranged system of mutual aids, I went up the school on co-operative principles.

How we—the originals of Stalky, M'Turk, and Beetle—first came together I do not remember, but our Triple Alliance was well established before we were thirteen. We had been oppressed by a large toughish boy who raided our poor little lockers. We took him on in a long, mixed rough-and-tumble, just this side of the real thing. At the end we were all-out (we worked by pressure and clinging, much as bees 'ball' a Queen) and he never troubled us again.

Turkey possessed an invincible detachment—far beyond mere insolence—towards all the world and a tongue, when he used it, dipped in some Irish-blue acid. Moreover, he spoke, sincerely, of the masters as 'ushers, ' which was not without charm. His general attitude was that of Ireland in English affairs at that time.

For executive capacity, the organisation of raids, reprisals, and retreats, we depended on Stalky, our Commander-in-Chief and Chief of his own Staff. He came of a household with a stern head, and, I fancy, had training in the holidays. Turkey never told us much about his belongings. He turned up, usually a day or two late, by the Irish packet, aloof, inscrutable, and contradictious. On him lay the burden of decorating our study, for he served a strange God called Ruskin. We fought among ourselves 'regular an' faithful as man an' wife, ' but any debt which we owed elsewhere was faithfully paid by all three of us.

Our 'socialisation of educational opportunities' took us unscathed up the school, till the original of Little Hartopp, asking one question too many, disclosed that I did not know what a cosine was and compared me to 'brute beasts. ' I taught Turkey all he ever knew of French, and he tried to make Stalky and me comprehend a little Latin. There is much to be said for this system, if you want a boy to learn anything, because he will remember what he gets from an equal where his master's words are forgotten. Similarly, when it was necessary to Stalky that I should get into the Choir, he taught me how to quaver 'I know a maiden fair to see' by punching me in the kidneys all up and down the cricket-field. (But some small trouble over a solitaire marble pushed from beneath the hem of a robe down the choir-steps into the tiled aisle ended that venture.)

I think it was his infernal impersonality that swayed us all in our wars and peace. He saw not only us but himself from the outside, and in later life, as we met in India and elsewhere, the gift persisted.

At long last, when with an equipment of doubtful Ford cars and a collection of most-mixed troops, he put up a monumental bluff against the Bolsheviks somewhere in Armenia (it is written in his Adventures of Dunsterforce) and was as nearly as possible destroyed, he wrote to the authorities responsible. I asked him what happened. 'They told me they had no more use for my services, ' said he. Naturally I condoled. 'Wrong as usual, ' said the ex-Head of Number Five study. 'If any officer under me had written what I did to the War Office, I'd have had him broke in two twos. ' That fairly sums up the man—and the boy who commanded us. I think I was a buffer state between his drivings and his tongue-lashings and his campaigns in which we were powers; and the acrid, devastating Turkey who, as I have written, 'lived and loved to destroy illusions' yet reached always after beauty. They took up room on tables that I wanted for writing; they broke into my reveries; they mocked my Gods; they stole, pawned or sold my outlying or neglected possessions; and—I could not have gone on a week without them nor they without me.

But my revenge was ample. I have said I was physically precocious. In my last term I had been thrusting an unlovely chin at C—— in form. At last he blew up, protested he could no longer abide the sight, and ordered me to shave. I carried this word to my House-master. He, who had long looked on me as a cultivated sink of iniquities, brooded over this confirmation of his suspicions, and gave me a written order on a Bideford barber for a razor, etc. I kindly invited my friends to come and help, and lamented for three miles the burden of compulsory shaving. There were no ripostes. There was no ribaldry. But why Stalky and Turkey did not cut their throats experimenting with the apparatus I do not understand.

We will now return to the savage life in which all these prodigious events 'transpired. '

We smoked, of course, but the penalties of discovery were heavy because the Prefects, who were all of the 'Army Class' up for the Sandhurst or Woolwich Preliminary, were allowed under restrictions to smoke pipes. If any of the rank and file were caught smoking, they came up before the Prefects, not on moral grounds, but for usurping the privileges of the Ruling Caste. The classic phrase was; 'You esteem yourself to be a Prefect, do you? All right. Come to my study at six, please. ' This seemed to work better than religious lectures and even expulsions which some establishments used to deal out for this dread sin.

Oddly enough 'fagging' did not exist, though the name 'fag' was regularly used as a term of contempt and sign of subordination against the Lower School. If one needed a 'varlet' to clean things in a study or run errands, that was a matter for private bargaining in our only currency—food. Sometimes such service gave protection, in the sense that it was distinct cheek to oppress an accredited 'varlet. ' I never served thus, owing to my untidiness; but our study entertained one sporadically, and to him we three expounded all housewifely duties. But, as a rule, Turkey would tidy up like the old maid to whom we always compared him.

Games were compulsory unless written excuse were furnished by competent authority. The penalty for wilful shirking was three cuts with a ground-ash from the Prefect of Games. One of the most difficult things to explain to some people is that a boy of seventeen or eighteen can thus beat a boy barely a year his junior, and on the heels of the punishment go for a walk with him; neither party bearing malice or pride.

So too in the War of '14 to '18 young gentlemen found it hard to understand that the Adjutant who poured vitriol on their heads at Parade, but was polite and friendly at Mess, was not sucking up to them to make amends for previous rudeness.

Except in the case of two House-masters I do not recall being lectured or preached at on morals or virtue. It is not always expedient to excite a growing youth's religious emotions, because one set of nerves seems to communicate with others, and Heaven knows what mines a 'pi-jaw' may touch off. But there were no doors to our bare windy dormitories, nor any sort of lock on the form-rooms. Our masters, with one exception who lived outside, were unmarried. The school buildings, originally cheap lodging-houses, made one straight bar against a hillside, and the boys circulated up and down in front of it. A penal battalion could not have been more perfectly policed, though that we did not realise. Mercifully we knew little outside the immediate burden of the day and the necessity for getting into the Army. I think, then, that when we worked we worked harder than most schools.

My House-master was deeply conscientious and cumbered about with many cares for his charges. What he accomplished thereby I know not. His errors sprang from pure and excessive goodness. Me and my companions he always darkly and deeply suspected. Realising this, we little beasts made him sweat, which he did on slight provocation.

My main interest as I grew older was C— —, my English and Classics Master, a rowing-man of splendid physique, and a scholar who lived in secret hope of translating Theocritus worthily. He had a violent temper, no disadvantage in handling boys used to direct speech, and a gift of schoolmaster's 'sarcasm' which must have been a relief to him and was certainly a treasure-trove to me. Also he was a good and House-proud House-master. Under him I came to feel that words could be used as weapons, for he did me the honour to talk at me plentifully; and our year-in year-out form-room bickerings gave us both something to play with. One learns more from a good scholar in a rage than from a score of lucid and laborious drudges; and to be made the butt of one's companions in full form is no bad preparation for later experiences. I think this 'approach' is now discouraged for fear of hurting the soul of youth, but in essence it is no more than rattling tins or firing squibs under a colt's nose. I remember nothing save satisfaction or envy when C— — broke his precious ointments over my head.

I tried to give a pale rendering of his style when heated in a 'Stalky' tale, 'Regulus, ' but I wish I could have presented him as he blazed forth once on the great Cleopatra Ode—the 27th of the Third Book. I had detonated him by a very vile construe of the first few lines. Having slain me, he charged over my corpse and delivered an interpretation of the rest of the Ode unequalled for power and insight. He held even the Army Class breathless.

There must be still masters of the same sincerity; and gramophone records of such good men, on the brink of profanity, struggling with a Latin form, would be more helpful to education than bushels of printed books. C— — taught me to loathe Horace for two years; to forget him for twenty, and then to love him for the rest of my days and through many sleepless nights.

After my second year at school, the tide of writing set in. In my holidays the three ladies listened—it was all I wanted—to anything I had to say. I drew on their books, from The City of Dreadful Night which shook me to my unformed core, Mrs. Gatty's Parables from Nature which I imitated and thought I was original, and scores of others. There were few atrocities of form or metre that I did not perpetrate and I enjoyed them all.

I discovered, also, that personal and well-pointed limericks on my companions worked well, and I and a red-nosed boy of uncertain temper exploited the idea—not without dust and heat; next, that the metre of Hiawatha saved one all bother about rhyme; and that there had been a man called Dante who, living in a small Italian town at general issue with his neighbours, had invented for most of them lively torments in a nine-ringed Hell, where he exhibited them to after-ages. C— — said, 'He must have made himself infernally unpopular. ' I combined my authorities.

I bought a fat, American-cloth-bound notebook, and set to work on an Inferno, into which I put, under appropriate torture, all my friends and most of the masters. This was really remunerative because one could chant his future doom to a victim walking below the windows of the study which I with my two companions now possessed. Then, 'as rare things will, ' my book vanished, and I lost interest in the Hiawatha metre.

Tennyson and Aurora Leigh came in the way of nature to me in the holidays, and C— — in form once literally threw Men and Women at my head. Here I found 'The Bishop orders his Tomb, ' 'Love among the Ruins' and 'Fra Lippo Lippi, ' a not too remote—I dare to think—ancestor of mine.

Swinburne's poems I must have come across first at the Aunt's. He did not strike my very young mind as 'anything in particular' till I read Atalanta in Calydon, and one verse of verses which exactly set the time for my side-stroke when I bathed in the big rollers off the Ridge. As thus: —

Who shall seek—thee and bring
　　And restore thee thy day [Half roll]
When the dove dipt her wing
　　And the oars won their way [Other half roll]
Where the narrowing Symplegades whitened
　　The Straits of Propontis with spray? [Carry on with the impetus]

If you can time the last line of it to end with a long roller crashing on your head, the cadence is complete. I even forgave Bret Harte, to whom I owed many things, for taking that metre in vain in his 'Heathen Chinee. ' But I never forgave C— — for bringing the fact to my notice.

Not till years later—talking things over with my 'Uncle Crom'—did I realise that injustices of this sort were not without intention. 'You needed a tight hand in those days, ' he drawled. 'C— — gave it to you. ' 'He did, ' said I, 'and so did H— —, ' the married master whom the school thoroughly feared.

'I remember that, ' Crom answered. 'Yes, that was me too. ' This had been an affair of an Essay—'A Day in the Holidays, ' or something of that nature. C— — had set it but the papers were to be marked by H— —. My essay was of variegated but constant vileness, modelled, I fancy, on holiday readings of a journal called The Pink 'Un. Even I had never done anything worse. Normally H— —'s markings would have been sent in to C— — without comment. On this occasion, however (I was in Latin form at the time), H— — entered and asked for the floor. C— — yielded it to him with a grin. H— — then told me off before my delighted companions in his best style, which was acid and contumelious. He wound up by a few general remarks about dying as a 'scurrilous journalist. ' (I think now that H—— too may have read The Pink 'Un.) The tone, matter, and setting of his discourse were as brutal as they were meant to be—brutal as the necessary wrench on the curb that fetches up a too-flippant colt. C—— added a rider or two after H—— had left.

(But it pleased Allah to afflict H—— in after years. I met him in charge of a 'mixed' College in New Zealand, where he taught a class of young ladies Latinity. 'And when they make false quantities, like you used to, they make-eyes at me! ' I thought of my chill mornings at Greek Testament under his ready hand, and pitied him from the bottom of my soul.)

Yes—I must have been 'nursed' with care by Crom and under his orders. Hence, when he saw I was irretrievably committed to the ink-pot, his order that I should edit the School Paper and have the run of his Library Study. Hence, I presume, C——'s similar permission, granted and withdrawn as the fortunes of our private war varied. Hence the Head's idea that I should learn Russian with him (I got as far as some of the cardinal numbers) and, later, précis-writing. This latter meant severe compression of dry-as-dust material, no essential fact to be omitted. The whole was sweetened with reminiscences of the men of Crom's youth, and throughout the low, soft drawl and the smoke of his perpetual Vevey he shed light on the handling of words. Heaven forgive me! I thought these privileges were due to my transcendent personal merits.

Many of us loved the Head for what he had done for us, but I owed him more than all of them put together; and I think I loved him even more than they did. There came a day when he told me that a fortnight after the close of the summer holidays of '82, I would go to India to work on a paper in Lahore, where my parents lived, and would get one hundred silver rupees a month! At term-end he most unjustly devised a prize poem—subject 'The Battle of Assaye ', which, there being no competitor, I won in what I conceived was the metre of my latest 'infection'—Joaquin Miller. And when I took the prize-book, Trevelyan's Competition Wallah, Crom Price said that if I went on I might be heard of again.

I spent my last few days before sailing with the beloved Aunt in the little cottage that the Burne-Jones' had bought for a holiday house at Rottingdean. There I looked across the village green and the horse-pond at a house called 'The Elms' behind a flint wall, and at a church opposite; and—had I known it—at 'The bodies of those to be In the Houses of Death and of Birth. '

Chapter III

Seven Years' Hard

I am poor Brother Lippo by your leave.
You need not clap your torches to my face.
                              Fra Lippo Lippi.

So, at sixteen years and nine months, but looking four or five years
older, and adorned with real whiskers which the scandalised Mother
abolished within one hour of beholding, I found myself at Bombay
where I was born, moving among sights and smells that made me
deliver in the vernacular sentences whose meaning I knew not.
Other Indian-born boys have told me how the same thing happened
to them.

There were yet three or four days' rail to Lahore, where my people
lived. After these, my English years fell away, nor ever, I think, came
back in full strength.

That was a joyous home-coming. For—consider! —I had returned to
a Father and Mother of whom I had seen but little since my sixth
year. I might have found my Mother 'the sort of woman I don't care
for, ' as in one terrible case that I know; and my Father intolerable.
But the Mother proved more delightful than all my imaginings or
memories. My Father was not only a mine of knowledge and help,
but a humorous, tolerant, and expert fellow-craftsman. I had my
own room in the house; my servant, handed over to me by my
father's servant, whose son he was, with the solemnity of a marriage-
contract; my own horse, cart, and groom; my own office-hours and
direct responsibilities; and—oh joy! —my own office-box, just like
my Father's, which he took daily to the Lahore Museum and School
of Art. I do not remember the smallest friction in any detail of our
lives. We delighted more in each other's society than in that of
strangers; and when my sister came out, a little later, our cup was
filled to the brim. Not only were we happy, but we knew it.

But the work was heavy. I represented fifty per cent of the 'editorial staff' of the one daily paper of the Punjab—a small sister of the great Pioneer at Allahabad under the same proprietorship. And a daily paper comes out every day even though fifty per cent of the staff have fever.

My Chief took me in hand, and for three years or so I loathed him. He had to break me in, and I knew nothing. What he suffered on my account I cannot tell; but the little that I ever acquired of accuracy, the habit of trying at least to verify references, and some knack of sticking to desk-work, I owed wholly to Stephen Wheeler.

I never worked less than ten hours and seldom more than fifteen per diem; and as our paper came out in the evening did not see the midday sun except on Sundays. I had fever too, regular and persistent, to which I added for a while chronic dysentery. Yet I discovered that a man can work with a temperature of 104, even though next day he has to ask the office who wrote the article. Our native Foreman, on the News side, Mian Rukn Din, a Muhammedan gentleman of kind heart and infinite patience, whom I never saw unequal to a situation, was my loyal friend throughout. From the modern point of view I suppose the life was not fit for a dog, but my world was filled with boys, but a few years older than I, who lived utterly alone, and died from typhoid mostly at the regulation age of twenty-two. As regarding ourselves at home, if there were any dying to be done, we four were together. The rest was in the day's work, with love to sweeten all things.

Books, plays, pictures, and amusements, outside what games the cold weather allowed, there were none. Transport was limited to horses and such railways as existed. This meant that one's normal radius of travel would be about six miles in any direction, and—one did not meet new white faces at every six miles. Death was always our near companion. When there was an outbreak of eleven cases of typhoid in our white community of seventy, and professional nurses had not been invented, the men sat up with the men and the women with the women. We lost four of our invalids and thought we had done well. Otherwise, men and women dropped where they stood.

Hence our custom of looking up any one who did not appear at our daily gatherings.

The dead of all times were about us—in the vast forgotten Muslim cemeteries round the Station, where one's horse's hoof of a morning might break through to the corpse below; skulls and bones tumbled out of our mud garden walls, and were turned up among the flowers by the Rains; and at every point were tombs of the dead. Our chief picnic rendezvous and some of our public offices had been memorials to desired dead women; and Fort Lahore, where Runjit Singh's wives lay, was a mausoleum of ghosts.

This was the setting in which my world revolved. Its centre for me—a member at seventeen—was the Punjab Club, where bachelors, for the most part, gathered to eat meals of no merit among men whose merits they knew well. My Chief was married and came there seldom, so it was mine to be told every evening of the faults of that day's issue in very simple language. Our native compositors 'followed copy' without knowing one word of English. Hence glorious and sometimes obscene misprints. Our proof-readers (sometimes we had a brace of them) drank, which was expected; but systematic and prolonged D. T. on their part gave me more than my share of their work. And in that Club and elsewhere I met none except picked men at their definite work—Civilians, Army, Education, Canals, Forestry, Engineering, Irrigation, Railways, Doctors, and Lawyers—samples of each branch and each talking his own shop. It follows then that that 'show of technical knowledge' for which I was blamed later came to me from the horse's mouth, even to boredom.

So soon as my paper could trust me a little, and I had behaved well at routine work, I was sent out, first for local reportings; then to race-meetings which included curious nights in the lottery-tent. (I saw one go up in flame once, when a heated owner hove an oil-lamp at the handicapper on the night the owner was coming up for election at the Club. That was the first and last time I had seen every available black ball expended and members begging for more.) Later I described openings of big bridges and such-like, which meant a night or two with the engineers; floods on railways—more nights in the wet with wretched heads of repair gangs; village festivals and consequent outbreaks of cholera or small-pox; communal riots under the shadow of the Mosque of Wazir Khan, where the patient waiting troops lay in timber-yards or side-alleys till the order came to go in and hit the crowds on the feet with the gun-butt (killing in Civil Administration was then reckoned confession of failure), and the growling, flaring, creed-drunk city would be brought to hand without effusion of blood, or the appearance of any agitated Viceroy; visits of Viceroys to neighbouring Princes on the edge of the great Indian Desert, where a man might have to wash his raw hands and face in soda-water; reviews of Armies expecting to move against Russia next week; receptions of an Afghan Potentate, with whom the Indian Government wished to stand well (this included a walk into the Khyber, where I was shot at, but without malice, by a rapparee who disapproved of his ruler's foreign policy); murder and divorce trials, and (a really filthy job) an inquiry into the percentage of lepers among the butchers who supplied beef and mutton to the European community of Lahore. (Here I first learned that crude statements of crude facts are not well-seen by responsible official authorities.) It was Squeers' method of instruction, but how could I fail to be equipped with more than all I might need? I was saturated with it, and if I tripped over detail, the Club attended to me.

My first bribe was offered to me at the age of nineteen when I was in a Native State where, naturally, one concern of the Administration was to get more guns of honour added to the Ruler's official salute when he visited British India, and even a roving correspondent's good word might be useful. Hence in the basket of fruits (dali is its name) laid at my tent door each morning, a five-hundred-rupee note and a Cashmere shawl. As the sender was of high caste I returned the gift at the hands of the camp-sweeper, who was not. Upon this my servant, responsible to his father, and mine, for my well-being, said without emotion; 'Till we get home you eat and drink from my hands. ' This I did.

On return to work I found my Chief had fever, and I was in sole charge. Among his editorial correspondence was a letter from this

Native State setting forth the record during a few days' visit of 'your reporter, a person called Kipling'; who had broken, it seemed, the Decalogue in every detail from rape to theft. I wrote back that as Acting-Editor I had received the complaints and would investigate, but they must expect me to be biassed because I was the person complained of.

I visited the State more than once later, and there was not a cloud on our relations. I had dealt with the insult more Asiatico—which they understood; the ball had been returned more Asiatico—which I understood; and the incident had been closed.

My second bribe came when I worked under Stephen Wheeler's successor, Kay Robinson, brother of Phil Robinson who wrote In My Indian Garden. With him, thanks to his predecessor having licked me into some shape, my relations were genial. It was the old matter of gun-salutes again; the old machinery of the basket of fruit and shawls and money for us both, but this time left impudently on the office verandah. Kay and I wasted a happy half-hour pricking 'Timeo Danaos et dona ferentes' into the currency notes, mourned that we could not take either them or the shawls, and let the matter go.

My third and most interesting bribe was when reporting a divorce case in Eurasian society. An immense brown woman penned me in a corner and offered 'if I would but keep her name out of it' to give me most intimate details, which she began at once to do. I demanded her name before bargaining. 'Oah! I am the Respondent. Thatt is why I ask you. ' It is hard to report some dramas without Ophelias if not Hamlets. But I was repaid for her anger when Counsel asked her if she had ever expressed a desire to dance on her husband's grave. Till then she had denied everything. 'Yess, ' she hissed, 'and I jolly-damn-well would too. '

A soldier of my acquaintance had been sentenced to life-imprisonment for a murder which, on evidence not before the court, seemed to me rather justified. I saw him later in Lahore gaol at work on some complicated arrangement of nibs with different coloured

28

inks, stuck into a sort of loom which, drawn over paper, gave the ruling for the blank forms of financial statements. It seemed wickedly monotonous. But the spirit of man is undefeatable. 'If I made a mistake of an eighth of an inch in spacing these lines, I'd throw out all the accounts of the Upper Punjab, ' said he.

As to our reading public, they were at the least as well educated as fifty per cent of our 'staff'; and by force of their lives could not be stampeded or much 'thrilled. ' Double headlines we had never heard of, nor special type, and I fear that the amount of 'white' in the newspapers to-day would have struck us as common cheating. Yet the stuff we dealt in would have furnished modern journals of enterprise with almost daily sensations.

My legitimate office-work was sub-editing, which meant eternal cuttings-down of unwieldy contributions—such as discourses on abstruse questions of Revenue and Assessment from a great and wise Civilian who wrote the vilest hand that even our compositors ever saw; literary articles about Milton. (And how was I to know that the writer was a relative of one of our proprietors, who thought our paper existed to air his theories?) Here Crom Price's training in précis-work helped me to get swiftly at what meat there might be in the disorderly messes. There were newspaper exchanges from Egypt to Hong-Kong to be skimmed nearly every morning and, once a week, the English papers on which one drew in time of need; local correspondence from outstations to vet for possible libels in their innocent allusions; 'spoofing' letters from subalterns to be guarded against (twice I was trapped here); always, of course, the filing of cables, and woe betide an error then! I took them down from the telephone—a primitive and mysterious power whose native operator broke every word into mono syllables. One cut-and-come-again affliction was an accursed Muscovite paper, the Novoie Vremya, written in French, which, for weeks and weeks, published the war diaries of Alikhanoff, a Russian General then harrying the Central Russian Khanates. He gave the name of every camp he halted at, and regularly reported that his troops warmed themselves at fires of sax-aul, which I suppose is perhaps sage-brush. A week after I had translated the last of the series every remembrance of it passed from my normal memory.

Ten or twelve years later, I fell sick in New York and passed through a long delirium which, by ill-chance, I remembered when I returned to life. At one stage of it I led an enormous force of cavalry mounted on red horses with brand-new leather saddles, under the glare of a green moon, across steppes so vast that they revealed the very curve of earth. We would halt at one of the camps named by Alikhanoff in his diary (I would see the name of it heaving up over the edge of the planet), where we warmed ourselves at fires of sax-aul, and where, scorched on one side and frozen on the other, I sat till my infernal squadrons went on again to the next fore-known halt; and so through the list.

In the early '80s a Liberal Government had come into power at Home and was acting on liberal 'principle, ' which so far as I have observed ends not seldom in bloodshed. Just then, it was a matter of principle that Native Judges should try white women. Native in this case meant overwhelmingly Hindu; and the Hindu's idea of women is not lofty. No one had asked for any such measure—least of all the Judiciary concerned. But principle is principle, though the streets swim. The European community were much annoyed. They went to the extremity of revolt—that is to say even the officials of the Service and their wives very often would not attend the functions and levees of the then Viceroy, a circular and bewildered recluse of religious tendencies. A pleasant English gentleman called C. P. Ilbert had been imported to father and god-father the Bill. I think he, too, was a little bewildered. Our paper, like most of the European Press, began with stern disapproval of the measure, and, I fancy, published much comment and correspondence which would now be called 'disloyal.'

One evening, while putting the paper to bed, I looked as usual over the leader. It was the sort of false-balanced, semi-judicial stuff that some English journals wrote about the Indian White Paper from 1932 to '34, and like them it furnished a barely disguised exposition of the Government's high ideals. In after-life one got to know that touch better, but it astonished me at the time, and I asked my Chief what it all meant. He replied, as I should have done in his place; 'None of your dam' business, ' and, being married, went to his home. I repaired to the Club which, remember, was the whole of my outside world.

As I entered the long, shabby dining-room where we all sat at one table, everyone hissed. I was innocent enough to ask; 'What's the joke? Who are they hissing? ' 'You, ' said the man at my side. 'Your dam' rag has ratted over the Bill. '

It is not pleasant to sit still when one is twenty while all your universe hisses you. Then uprose a Captain, our Adjutant of Volunteers, and said: 'Stop that! The boy's only doing what he's paid to do. ' The demonstration tailed off, but I had seen a great light. The Adjutant was entirely correct. I was a hireling, paid to do what I was paid to do, and—I did not relish the idea. Someone said kindly; 'You damned young ass! Don't you know that your paper has the Government printing-contract? ' I did know it, but I had never before put two and two together.

A few months later one of my two chief proprietors received the decoration that made him a Knight. Then I began to take much interest in certain smooth Civilians, who had seen good in the Government measure and had somehow been shifted out of the heat to billets in Simla. I followed under shrewd guidance, often native, the many pretty ways by which a Government can put veiled pressure on its employees in a land where every circumstance and relation of a man's life is public property. So, when the great and epoch-making India Bill turned up fifty years later, I felt as one re-treading the tortuous byways of his youth. One recognised the very phrases and assurances of the old days still doing good work, and waited, as in a dream, for the very slightly altered formulas in which those who were parting with their convictions excused themselves. Thus; 'I may act as a brake, you know. At any rate I'm keeping a more extreme man out of the game. ' 'There's no sense running counter to the inevitable, '—and all the other Devil-provided camouflage for the sinner-who-faces-both-ways.

In '85 I was made a Freemason by dispensation (Lodge Hope and Perseverance 782 E. C.), being under age, because the Lodge hoped for a good Secretary. They did not get him, but I helped, and got the Father to advise, in decorating the bare walls of the Masonic Hall with hangings after the prescription of Solomon's Temple. Here I met Muslims, Hindus, Sikhs, members of the Arya and Brahmo Samaj, and a Jew tyler, who was priest and butcher to his little community in the city. So yet another world opened to me which I needed.

My Mother and sister would go up to the Hills for the hot weather, and in due course my Father too. My own holiday came when I could be spared. Thus I often lived alone in the big house, where I commanded by choice native food, as less revolting than meat-cookery, and so added indigestion to my more intimate possessions.

In those months—mid-April to mid-October—one took up one's bed and walked about with it from room to room, seeking for less heated air; or slept on the flat roof with the waterman to throw half-skinfuls of water on one's parched carcase. This brought on fever but saved heat-stroke.

Often the night got into my head as it had done in the boarding-house in the Brompton Road, and I would wander till dawn in all manner of odd places-liquor-shops, gambling-and opium-dens, which are not a bit mysterious, wayside entertainments such as puppet-shows, native dances; or in and about the narrow gullies under the Mosque of Wazir Khan for the sheer sake of looking. Sometimes, the Police would challenge, but I knew most of their officers, and many folk in some quarters knew me for the son of my Father, which in the East more than anywhere else is useful. Otherwise, the word 'Newspaper' sufficed; though I did not supply my paper with many accounts of these prowls. One would come home, just as the light broke, in some night-hawk of a hired carriage which stank of hookah-fumes, jasmine-flowers, and sandalwood; and if the driver were moved to talk, he told one a good deal. Much of real Indian life goes on in the hot-weather nights. That is why the native staff of the offices are not much use next morning. All native offices aestivate from May at least till September. Files and correspondence are then as a matter of course pitched unopened into corners, to be written up or faked when the weather gets cooler. But the English who go Home on leave, having imposed the set hours of a northern working day upon the children of children, are surprised that India does not work as they do. This is one of the reasons why autonomous India will be interesting.

And there were 'wet' nights too at the Club or one Mess, when a tableful of boys, half-crazed with discomfort, but with just sense enough to stick to beer and bones which seldom betray, tried to rejoice and somehow succeeded. I remember one night when we ate tinned haggis with cholera in the cantonments 'to see what would happen, ' and another when a savage stallion in harness was presented with a very hot leg of roast mutton, as he snapped. Theoretically this is a cure for biting, but it only made him more of a cannibal.

I got to meet the soldiery of those days in visits to Fort Lahore and, in a less degree, at Mian Mir Cantonments. My first and best beloved Battalion was the 2nd Fifth Fusiliers, with whom I dined in awed silence a few weeks after I came out. When they left I took up with their successors, the 30th East Lancashire, another North-country regiment; and, last, with the 31st East Surrey—a London recruited confederacy of skilful dog-stealers, some of them my good and loyal friends. There were ghostly dinners too with Subalterns in charge of the Infantry Detachment at Fort Lahore, where, all among marble-inlaid, empty apartments of dead Queens, or under the domes of old tombs, meals began with the regulation thirty grains of quinine in the sherry, and ended—as Allah pleased!

I am, by the way, one of the few civilians who have turned out a Quarter-Guard of Her Majesty's troops. It was on a chill winter morn, about 2 A. M. at the Fort, and though I suppose I had been given the countersign on my departure from the Mess, I forgot it ere I reached the Main Guard, and when challenged announced myself spaciously as 'Visiting Rounds. ' When the men had clattered out I asked the Sergeant if he had ever seen a finer collection of scoundrels. That cost me beer by the gallon, but it was worth it.

Having no position to consider, and my trade enforcing it, I could move at will in the fourth dimension. I came to realise the bare horrors of the private's life, and the unnecessary torments he endured on account of the Christian doctrine which lays down that 'the wages of sin is death. ' It was counted impious that bazaar prostitutes should be inspected; or that the men should be taught elementary precautions in their dealings with them. This official virtue cost our Army in India nine thousand expensive white men a year always laid up from venereal disease. Visits to Lock Hospitals made me desire, as earnestly as I do to-day, that I might have six hundred priests — Bishops of the Establishment for choice — to handle for six months precisely as the soldiers of my youth were handled.

Heaven knows the men died fast enough from typhoid, which seemed to have something to do with water, but we were not sure; or from cholera, which was manifestly a breath of the Devil that could kill all on one side of a barrack-room and spare the others; from seasonal fever; or from what was described as 'blood-poisoning. '

Lord Roberts, at that time Commander-in-Chief in India, who knew my people, was interested in the men, and — I had by then written one or two stories about soldiers — the proudest moment of my young life was when I rode up Simla Mall beside him on his usual explosive red Arab, while he asked me what the men thought about their accommodation, entertainment-rooms and the like. I told him, and he thanked me as gravely as though I had been a full Colonel.

My month's leave at Simla, or whatever Hill Station my people went to, was pure joy — every golden hour counted. It began in heat and discomfort, by rail and road. It ended in the cool evening, with a wood fire in one's bedroom, and next morn — thirty more of them ahead! — the early cup of tea, the Mother who brought it in, and the long talks of us all together again. One had leisure to work, too, at whatever play-work was in one's head, and that was usually full.

Simla was another new world. There the Hierarchy lived, and one saw and heard the machinery of administration stripped bare. There were the Heads of the Viceregal and Military staffs and their Aides-de-Camp; and playing whist with Great Ones, who gave him special news, was the Correspondent of our big sister paper the Pioneer, then a power in the land.

The dates, but not the pictures, of those holidays are blurred. At one time our little world was full of the aftermaths of Theosophy as taught by Madame Blavatsky to her devotees. My Father knew the lady and, with her, would discuss wholly secular subjects; she being, he told me, one of the most interesting and unscrupulous impostors he had ever met. This, with his experience, was a high compliment. I was not so fortunate, but came across queer, bewildered, old people, who lived in an atmosphere of 'manifestations' running about their houses. But the earliest days of Theosophy devastated the Pioneer, whose Editor became a devout believer, and used the paper for propaganda to an extent which got on the nerves not only of the public but of a proof-reader, who at the last moment salted an impassioned leader on the subject with, in brackets; 'What do you bet this is a dam' lie? ' The Editor was most untheosophically angry!

On one of my Simla leaves—I had been ill with dysentery again—I was sent off for rest along the Himalaya-Tibet road in the company of an invalid officer and his wife. My equipment was my servant— he from whose hands I had fed in the Native State before-mentioned; Dorothea Darbishoff, alias Dolly Bobs, a temperamental she-pony; and four baggage-coolies who were recruited and changed at each stage. I knew the edge of the great Hills both from Simla and Dalhousie, but had never marched any distance into them. They were to me a revelation of 'all might, majesty, dominion, and power, henceforth and for ever, ' in colour, form, and substance indescribable. A little of what I realised then came back to me in Kim.

On the day I turned back for Simla—my companions were going further—my servant embroiled himself with a new quartette of coolies and managed to cut the eye of one of them. I was a few score miles from the nearest white man, and did not wish to be haled before any little Hill Rajah, knowing as I did that the coolies would unitedly swear that I had directed the outrage. I therefore paid blood-money, and strategically withdrew — on foot for the most part because Dolly Bobs objected to every sight and most of the smells of the landscape. I had to keep the coolies who, like the politicians, would not stay put, in front of me on the six-foot-wide track, and, as is ever the case when one is in difficulties, it set in to rain. My urgent business was to make my first three days' march in one — a matter of thirty odd miles. My coolies wanted to shy off to their village and spend their ill-gotten silver. On me developed the heartbreaking job of shepherding a retreat. I do not think my mileage that day could have been much less than forty miles of sheer up-hill and down-dale slogging. But it did me great good, and enabled me to put away bottles of strong Army beer at the wet evening's end in the resthouse. On our last day, a thunderstorm, which had been at work a few thousand feet below us, rose to the level of the ridge we were crossing and exploded in our midst. We were all flung on our faces, and when I was able to see again I observed the half of a well-grown pine, as neatly split lengthwise as a match by a penknife, in the act of hirpling down the steep hillside by itself. The thunder drowned everything, so that it seemed to be posturing in dumb show, and when it began to hop — horrible vertical hops — the effect was of pure D. T. My coolies, however, who had had the tale of my misdeeds from their predecessors, argued that if the local Gods missed such a sitting shot as I had given them, I could not be altogether unlucky.

It was on this trip that I saw a happy family of four bears out for a walk together, all talking at the tops of their voices; and also — the sun on his wings, a thousand feet below me — I stared long at a wheeling eagle, himself thousands of feet above the map-like valley he was quartering.

On my return I handed my servant over to his father, who dealt faithfully with him for having imperilled my Father's son. But what I did not tell him was that my servant, a Punjabi Muslim, had in his first panic embraced the feet of the injured hill-coolie, a heathen, and begged him to 'show mercy. ' A servant, precisely because he is a servant, has his izzat—his honour—or, as the Chinese say, his 'face. ' Save that, and he is yours. One should never rate one's man before others; nor, if he knows that you know the implication of the words that you are using on him, should you ever use certain words and phrases. But to a young man raw from England, or to an old one in whose service one has grown grey, anything is permitted. In the first case; 'He is a youngster. He slangs as his girl has taught him, ' and the man keeps his countenance even though his master's worst words are inflected woman-fashion. In the second case, the aged servitor and deputy-conscience says; 'It is naught. We were young men together. Ah! you should have heard him then! '

The reward for this very small consideration is service of a kind that one accepted as a matter of course—till one was without it. My man would go monthly to the local Bank and draw my pay in coined rupees, which he would carry home raw in his waist-band, as the whole bazaar knew, and decant into an old wardrobe, whence I would draw for my needs till there remained no more.

Yet, it was necessary to his professional honour that he should present me monthly a list of petty disbursements on my personal behalf—such as oil for the buggy-lamps, bootlaces, thread for darning my socks, buttons replaced and the like—all written out in bazaar-English by the letter-writer at the corner of the road. The total rose, of course, with my pay, and on each rupee of this bill my man took the commission of the East, say one-sixteenth or perhaps one-tenth of each rupee.

For the rest, till I was in my twenty-fourth year, I no more dreamed of dressing myself than I did of shutting an inner door or—I was going to say turning a key in a lock. But we had no locks. I gave myself indeed the trouble of stepping into the garments that were held out to me after my bath, and out of them as I was assisted to do. And—luxury of which I dream still—I was shaved before I was awake!

One must set these things against the taste of fever in one's mouth, and the buzz of quinine in one's ears; the temper frayed by heat to breakingpoint but for sanity's sake held back from the break; the descending darkness of intolerable dusks; and the less supportable dawns of fierce, stale heat through half of the year.

When my people were at the Hills and I was alone, my Father's butler took command. One peril of solitary life is going to seed in details of living. As our numbers at the Club shrank between April and mid-September, men grew careless, till at last our conscience-stricken Secretary, himself an offender, would fetch us up with a jerk, and forbid us dining in little more than singlet and riding-breeches.

This temptation was stronger in one's own house, though one knew if one broke the ritual of dressing for the last meal one was parting with a sheet-anchor. (Young gentlemen of larger views to-day consider this 'dress-for-dinner' business as an affectation ranking with 'the old school tie. '—I would give some months' pay for the privilege of enlightening them.) Here the butler would take charge. 'For the honour of the house there must be a dinner. It is long since the Sahib has bidden friends to eat. ' I would protest like a fretful child. He would reply; 'Except for the names of the Sahibs to be invited all things are on my head. ' So one dug up four or five companions in discomfort; the pitiful, scorched marigold blooms would appear on the table and, to a full accompaniment of glass, silver, and napery, the ritual would be worked through, and the butler's honour satisfied for a while.

At the Club, sudden causeless hates flared up between friends and died down like straw fires; old grievances were recalled and brooded over aloud; the complaint-book bristled with accusations and inventions. All of which came to nothing when the first Rains fell, and after a three days' siege of creeping and crawling things, whose bodies stopped our billiards and almost put out the lamps they sizzled in, life picked up in the blessed cool.

But it was a strange life. Once, suddenly, in the Club ante-room a man asked a neighbour to pass him the newspaper. 'Get it yourself, ' was the hot-weather answer. The man rose but on his way to the table dropped and writhed in the first grip of cholera. He was carried to his quarters, the Doctor came, and for three days he went through all the stages of the disease even to the characteristic baring of discoloured gums. Then he returned to life and, on being condoled with, said; 'I remember getting up to get the paper, but after that, give you my word, I don't remember a thing till I heard Lawrie say that I was coming out of it. ' I have heard since that oblivion is sometimes vouchsafed.

Though I was spared the worst horrors, thanks to the pressure of work, a capacity for being able to read, and the pleasure of writing what my head was filled with, I felt each succeeding hot weather more and more, and cowered in my soul as it returned.

This is fit place for a 'pivot' experience to be set side by side with the affair of the Adjutant of Volunteers at the Club. It happened one hotweather evening, in '86 or thereabouts, when I felt that I had come to the edge of all endurance. As I entered my empty house in the dusk there was no more in me except the horror of a great darkness, that I must have been fighting for some days. I came through that darkness alive, but how I do not know. Late at night I picked up a book by Walter Besant which was called All in a Garden Fair. It dealt with a young man who desired to write; who came to realise the possibilities of common things seen, and who eventually succeeded in his desire. What its merits may be from today's 'literary' standpoint I do not know. But I do know that that book was my salvation in sore personal need, and with the reading and re-reading it became to me a revelation, a hope and strength. I was certainly, I argued, as well equipped as the hero and—and—after all, there was no need for me to stay here for ever. I could go away and measure myself against the doorsills of London as soon as I had money. Therefore I would begin to save money, for I perceived there was absolutely no reason outside myself why I should not do exactly what to me seemed good. For proof of my revelation I did, sporadically but sincerely, try to save money, and I built up in my head—always with the book to fall back upon—a dream of the future that sustained me. To Walter Besant singly and solely do I owe this—as I told him when we met, and he laughed, rolled in his chair, and seemed pleased.

In the joyous reign of Kay Robinson, my second Chief, our paper changed its shape and type. This took up for a week or so all hours of the twenty-four and cost me a break-down due to lack of sleep. But we two were proud of the results. One new feature was a daily 'turnover'—same as the little pink Globe at Home—of one column and a quarter. Naturally, the 'office' had to supply most of them and once more I was forced to 'write short. '

All the queer outside world would drop into our workshop sooner or later—say a Captain just cashiered for horrible drunkenness, who reported his fall with a wry, appealing face, and then—disappeared. Or a man old enough to be my father, on the edge of tears because he had been overpassed for Honours in the Gazette. Or three troopers of the Ninth Lancers, one of whom was an old schoolmate of mine who became a General with an expedition of his own in West Africa in the Great War. The other two also were gentlemen-rankers who rose to high commands. One met men going up and down the ladder in every shape of misery and success.

There was a night at the Club when some silly idiot found a half-dead viper and brought it to dinner in a pickle-bottle. One man of the company kept messing about with the furious little beast on the table-cloth till he had to be warned to take his hands away. A few weeks after, some of us realised it would have been better had he accomplished what had been in his foreboding mind that night.

But the cold weather brought ample amends. The family were together again and—except for my Mother's ukase against her men bringing bound volumes of the Illustrated London News to meals (a survival of hot-weather savagery)—all was bliss. So, in the cold weather of '85 we four made up a Christmas annual called Quartette, which pleased us a great deal and attracted a certain amount of attention. (Later, much later, it became a 'collector's piece' in the U. S. bookmarket, and to that extent smudged the happy memories of its birth.) In '85 I began a series of tales in the Civil and Military Gazette which were called Plain Tales from the Hills. They came in when and as padding was needed. In '86 also I published a collection of newspaper verses on Anglo-Indian life, called Departmental Ditties, which, dealing with things known and suffered by many people, were well received. I had been allowed, further, to send stuff that we, editorially, had no use for, to far-off Calcutta papers, such as the Indigo Planters' Gazette, and elsewhere. These things were making for me the beginnings of a name even unto Bengal.

But mark how discreetly the cards were being dealt me. Up till '87 my performances had been veiled in the decent obscurity of the far end of an outlying province, among a specialised community who did not interest any but themselves. I was like a young horse entered for small, up-country events where I could get used to noise and crowds, fall about till I found my feet, and learn to keep my head with the hoofs drumming behind me. Better than all, the pace of my office-work was 'too good to inquire, ' and its nature—that I should realise all sorts and conditions of men and make others realise them—gave me no time to 'realise' myself.

Here was my modest notion of my own position at the end of my five years' Viceroyalty on the little Civil and Military Gazette. I was still fifty per cent of the editorial staff, though for a while I rose to have a man under me. But just are the Gods! —that varlet was 'literary' and must needs write Elia-like 'turnovers' instead of sticking to the legitimate! Any fool, I knew to my sorrow, could write. My job was to sub-edit him or her into some sort of shape. Any other fool could review; (I myself on urgent call have reviewed the later works of a writer called Browning, and what my Father said about that was unpublishable). Reporting was a minor 'feature, ' although we did not use that word. I myself qua reporter could turn in stuff one day and qua subeditor knock it remorselessly into cocked hats the next. The difference, then, between me and the vulgar herd who 'write for papers' was, as I saw it, the gulf that divides the beneficed clergyman from ladies and gentlemen who contribute pumpkins and dahlias to Harvest Festival decorations. To say that I magnified my office is to understate. But this may have saved me from magnifying myself beyond decency.

In '87 orders came for me to serve on the Pioneer, our big sister-paper at Allahabad, hundreds of miles to the southward, where I should be one of four at least and a new boy at a big school.

But the North-West Provinces, as they were then, being largely Hindu, were strange 'air and water' to me. My life had lain among Muslims, and a man leans one way or other according to his first service. The large, well-appointed Club, where Poker had just driven out Whist and men gambled seriously, was full of large-bore officials, and of a respectability all new. The Fort where troops were quartered had its points; but one bastion jutted out into a most holy river. Therefore, partially burned corpses made such a habit of stranding just below the Subalterns' quarters that a special expert was entertained to pole them off and onward. In Fort Lahore we dealt in nothing worse than ghosts.

Moreover, the Pioneer lived under the eye of its chief proprietor, who spent several months of each year in his bungalow over the way. It is true that I owed him my chance in life, but when one has been second in command of even a third-class cruiser, one does not care to have one's Admiral permanently moored at a cable's length. His love for his paper, which his single genius and ability had largely created, led him sometimes to 'give the boys a hand. ' On those hectic days (for he added and subtracted to the last minute) we were relieved when the issue caught the down-country mail.

But he was patient with me, as were the others, and through him again I got a wider field for 'outside stuff. ' There was to be a weekly edition of the Pioneer for Home consumption. Would I edit it, additional to ordinary work? Would I not? There would be fiction—syndicated serial-matter bought by the running foot from agencies at Home. That would fill one whole big page. The 'sight of means to do ill deeds' had the usual effect. Why buy Bret Harte, I asked, when I was prepared to supply home-grown fiction on the hoof? And I did.

My editing of the Weekly may have been a shade casual—it was but a re-hash of news and views after all. My head was full of, to me, infinitely more important material. Henceforth no mere twelve-hundred Plain Tales jammed into rigid frames, but three- or five-thousand-word cartoons once a week. So did young Lippo Lippi, whose child I was, look on the blank walls of his monastery when he was bidden decorate them 'Twas 'ask and have; Choose, for more's ready, ' with a vengeance.

I fancy my change of surroundings and outlook precipitated the rush. At the beginning of it I had an experience which, in my innocence, I mistook for the genuine motions of my Daemon. I must have been loaded more heavily than I realised with 'Gyp, ' for there came to me in scenes as stereoscopically clear as those in the crystal an Anglo-Indian Autour du Mariage. My pen took charge and I, greatly admiring, watched it write for me far into the nights. The result I christened The Story of the Gadsbys, and when it first appeared in England I was complimented on my 'knowledge of the world. ' After my indecent immaturity came to light, I heard less of these gifts. Yet, as the Father said loyally; 'It wasn't all so dam' bad, Ruddy. '

At any rate it went into the Weekly, together with soldier tales, Indian tales, and tales of the opposite sex. There was one of this last which, because of a doubt, I handed up to the Mother, who abolished it and wrote me; Never you do that again. But I did and managed to pull off, not unhandily, a tale called 'A Wayside Comedy, ' where I worked hard for a certain 'economy of implication, ' and in one phrase of less than a dozen words believed I had succeeded. More than forty years later a Frenchman, browsing about some of my old work, quoted this phrase as the clou of the tale and the key to its method. It was a belated 'workshop compliment' that I appreciated. Thus, then, I made my own experiments in the weights, colours, perfumes, and attributes of words in relation to other words, either as read aloud so that they may hold the ear, or, scattered over the page, draw the eye. There is no line of my verse or prose which has not been mouthed till the tongue has made all smooth, and memory, after many recitals, has mechanically skipped the grosser superfluities.

These things occupied and contented me, but—outside of them—I felt that I did not quite fit the Pioneer's scheme of things and that my superiors were of the same opinion. My work on the Weekly was not legitimate journalism. My flippancy in handling what I was trusted with was not well-seen by the Government or the departmental officialism, on which the Pioneer rightly depended for advance and private news, gathered in at Simla or Calcutta by our most important Chief Correspondent. I fancy my owners thought me safer on the road than in my chair; for they sent me out to look at Native State mines, mills, factories and the like. Here I think they were entirely justified. My proprietor at Allahabad had his own game to play (it brought him his well-deserved knighthood in due course) and, to some extent, my vagaries might have embarrassed him. One, I know, did. The Pioneer editorially, but cautiously as a terrier drawing up to a porcupine, had hinted that some of Lord Roberts' military appointments at that time verged on nepotism. It was a regretful and well-balanced allocution. My rhymed comment (and why my Chief passed it I know not!) said just the same thing, but not quite so augustly. All I remember of it are the last two flagrant lines:

And if the Pioneer is wrath
Oh Lord, what must you be!

I don't think Lord Roberts was pleased with it, but I know he was not half so annoyed as my chief proprietor.

On my side I was ripe for change and, thanks always to All in a Garden Fair, had a notion now of where I was heading. My absorption in the Pioneer Weekly stories, which I wanted to finish, had put my plans to the back of my head, but when I came out of that furious spell of work towards the end of '88 I rearranged myself. I wanted money for the future. I counted my assets. They came to one book of verse; one ditto prose; and—thanks to the Pioneer's permission—a set of six small paper-backed railway-bookstall volumes embodying most of my tales in the Weekly—copyright of which the Pioneer might well have claimed. The man who then controlled the Indian railway bookstalls came of an imaginative race, used to taking chances. I sold him the six paper-backed books for

£200 and a small royalty. Plain Tales from the Hills I sold for £50, and I forget how much the same publisher gave me for Departmental Ditties. (This was the first and last time I ever dealt direct with publishers.)

Fortified with this wealth, and six months' pay in lieu of notice, I left India for England by way of the Far East and the United States, after six and a half years of hard work and a reasonable amount of sickness. My God-speed came from the managing director, a gentleman of sound commercial instincts, who had never concealed his belief that I was grossly overpaid, and who, when he paid me my last wages, said; 'Take it from me, you'll never be worth more than four hundred rupees a month to anyone. ' Common pride bids me tell that at that time I was drawing seven hundred a month.

Accounts were squared between us curiously soon. When my notoriety fell upon me, there was a demand for my old proofs, signed and unsigned stuff not included in my books, and a general turning-out of refuse-bins for private publication and sale. This upset my hopes of editing my books decently and responsibly, and wrought general confusion. But I was told later that the Pioneer had made as much out of its share in this remnant-traffic as it had paid me in wages since I first landed. (Which shows how one cannot get ahead of gentlemen of sound commercial instincts.)

Yet a man must needs love anything that he has worked and suffered under. When, at long last, the Pioneer—India's greatest and most important paper which used to pay twenty-seven per cent to its shareholders—fell on evil days and, after being bedevilled and bewitched, was sold to a syndicate, and I received a notification beginning; 'We think you may be interested to know that, ' etc., I felt curiously alone and unsponsored. But my first mistress and most true love, the little Civil and Military Gazette, weathered the storm. Even if I wrote them, these lines are true: —

Something of Myself: For My Friends Known and Unknown

Try as he will, no man breaks wholly loose
    From his first love, no matter who she be.
Oh, was there ever sailor free to choose,
    That didn't settle somewhere near the sea?

Parsons in pulpits, tax-payers in pews,
    Kings on your thrones, you know as well as me,
We've only one virginity to lose,
    And where we lost it there our hearts will be!

And, besides, there is, or was, a tablet in my old Lahore office asserting that here I 'worked. ' And Allah knows that is true also!

Chapter IV

The Interregnum

The youth who daily farther from the East
Must travel . ..
    Wordsworth.

And, in the autumn of '89, I stepped into a sort of waking dream when I took, as a matter of course, the fantastic cards that Fate was pleased to deal me.

The ancient landmarks of my boyhood still stood. There were the beloved Aunt and Uncle, the little house of the Three Old Ladies, and in one corner of it the quiet figure by the fireplace composedly writing her next novel on her knee. It was at the quietest of tea-parties, in this circle, that I first met Mary Kingsley, the bravest woman of all my knowledge. We talked a good deal over the cups, and more while walking home afterwards—she of West African cannibals and the like. At last, the world forgetting, I said 'Come up to my rooms and we'll talk it out there. ' She agreed, as a man would, then suddenly remembering said; 'Oh, I forgot I was a woman. 'Fraid I mustn't. ' So I realised that my world was all to explore again.

A few—a very few—people in it had died, but no one expected to do so for another twenty years. White women stood and waited on one behind one's chair. It was all whirlingly outside my comprehension.

But my small stock-in-trade of books had become known in certain quarters; and there was an evident demand for my stuff. I do not recall that I stirred a hand to help myself. Things happened to me. I went, by invitation, to Mowbray Morris the editor of Macmillan's Magazine, who asked me how old I was and, when I told him I hoped to be twenty-four at the end of the year, said; 'Good God! ' He took from me an Indian tale and some verses, which latter he wisely edited a little. They were both published in the same number of the

Magazine—one signed by my name and the other 'Yussuf' All of this confirmed the feeling (which has come back at intervals through my life), 'Lord ha' mercy on me, this is none of I. '

Then more tales were asked for, and the editor of the St. James's Gazette wanted stray articles, signed and unsigned. My 'turnover' training on the Civil and Military made this easy for me, and somehow I felt easier with a daily paper under my right elbow.

About this time was an interview in a weekly paper, where I felt myself rather on the wrong side of the counter and that I ought to be questioning my questioner. Shortly after, that same weekly made me a proposition which I could not see my way to accept, and then announced that I was 'feeling my oats, ' of which, it was careful to point out, it had given me my first sieveful. Since, at that time, I was overwhelmed, not to say scared, by the amazing luck that had come to me, the pronouncement gave me confidence. If that was how I struck the external world—good! For naturally I considered the whole universe was acutely interested in me only—just as a man who strays into a skirmish is persuaded he is the pivot of the action.

Meantime, I had found me quarters in Villiers Street, Strand, which forty-six years ago was primitive and passionate in its habits and population. My rooms were small, not over-clean or well-kept, but from my desk I could look out of my window through the fanlight of Gatti's Music-Hall entrance, across the street, almost on to its stage. The Charing Cross trains rumbled through my dreams on one side, the boom of the Strand on the other, while, before my windows, Father Thames under the Shot Tower walked up and down with his traffic.

At the outset I had so muddled and mismanaged my affairs that, for a while, I found myself with some money owing me for work done, but no funds in hand. People who ask for money, however justifiably, have it remembered against them. The beloved Aunt, or any one of the Three Old Ladies, would have given to me without question; but that seemed too like confessing failure at the outset. My rent was paid; I had my dress-suit; I had nothing to pawn save a collection of unmarked shirts picked up in all the ports; so I made shift to manage on what small cash I had in pocket.

My rooms were above an establishment of Harris the Sausage King, who, for tuppence, gave as much sausage and mash as would carry one from breakfast to dinner when one dined with nice people who did not eat sausage for a living. Another tuppence found me a filling supper. The excellent tobacco of those days was, unless you sank to threepenny 'Shag' or soared to sixpenny 'Turkish, ' tuppence the half-ounce; and fourpence, which included a pewter of beer or porter, was the price of admission to Gatti's.

It was here, in the company of an elderly but upright barmaid from a pub near by, that I listened to the observed and compelling songs of the Lion and Mammoth Comiques, and the shriller strains—but equally 'observed'—of the Bessies and Bellas, whom I could hear arguing beneath my window with their cab-drivers, as they sped from Hall to Hall. One lady sometimes delighted us with viva-voce versions of—'what 'as just 'appened to me outside 'ere, if you'll believe it. ' Then she would plunge into brilliant improvisations. Oh, we believed! Many of us had, perhaps, taken part in the tail of that argument at the doors, ere she stormed in.

Those monologues I could never hope to rival, but the smoke, the roar, and the good-fellowship of relaxed humanity at Gatti's 'set' the scheme for a certain sort of song. The Private Soldier in India I thought I knew fairly well. His English brother (in the Guards mostly) sat and sang at my elbow any night I chose; and, for Greek chorus, I had the comments of my barmaid—deeply and dispassionately versed in all knowledge of evil as she had watched it across the zinc she was always swabbing off. (Hence, some years later, verses called 'Mary, pity Women, ' based on what she told me about 'a friend o' mine 'oo was mistook in 'er man. ') The outcome was the first of some verses called Barrack-Room Ballads which I showed to Henley of the Scots, later National Observer, who wanted more; and I became for a while one of the happy company who used to gather in a little restaurant off Leicester Square and regulate all literature till all hours of the morning.

I had the greatest admiration for Henley's verse and prose and, if such things be merchandise in the next world, will cheerfully sell a large proportion of what I have written for a single meditation—illumination—inspiration or what you please—that he wrote on the Arabian Nights in a tiny book of Essays and Reviews.

As regards his free verse I—plus some Chianti—once put forward the old notion that free verse was like fishing with barbless hooks. Henley replied volcanically. It was, said he, 'the cadences that did it. ' That was true; but he alone, to my mind, could handle them aright, being a Master Craftsman who had paid for his apprenticeship.

Henley's demerits were, of course, explained to the world by loving friends after his death. I had the fortune to know him only as kind, generous, and a jewel of an editor, with the gift of fetching the very best out of his cattle, with words that would astonish oxen. He had, further, an organic loathing of Mr. Gladstone and all Liberalism. A Government Commission of Enquiry was sitting in those days on some unusually blatant traffic in murder among the Irish Land Leaguers; and had whitewashed the whole crowd. Where upon, I wrote some impolite verses called 'Cleared! ' which at first The Times seemed ready to take but on second thoughts declined. I was recommended to carry them to a monthly review of sorts edited by a Mr. Frank Harris, whom I discovered to be the one human being that I could on no terms get on with. He, too, shied at the verses, which I referred to Henley, who, having no sense of political decency, published them in his Observer, and—after a cautious interval—The Times quoted them in full. This was rather like some of my experiences in India, and gave me yet more confidence.

To my great pride I was elected a Member of the Savile—'the little Savile' then in Piccadilly—and, on my introduction, dined with no less than Hardy and Walter Besant. My debts to the latter grew at once, and you may remember that I owed him much indeed. He had his own views on publishers, and was founding, or had just founded, the Authors' Society. He advised me to entrust my business to an agent and sent me to his own—A. P. Watt, whose son was about my own age. The father took hold of my affairs at once and most sagely; and on his death his son succeeded. In the course of forty odd years I do not recall any difference between us that three minutes' talk could not clear up. This, also, I owed to Besant.

Nor did his goodness halt there. He would sit behind his big, frosted beard and twinkling spectacles, and deal me out wisdom concerning this new incomprehensible world. One heard very good talk at the Savile. Much of it was the careless give-and-take of the atelier when the models are off their stands, and one throws bread-pellets at one's betters, and makes hay of all schools save one's own. But Besant saw deeper. He advised me to 'keep out of the dog-fight. ' He said that if I were 'in with one lot' I would have to be out with another; and that, at last, 'things would get like a girls' school where they stick out their tongues at each other when they pass. ' That was true too. One heard men vastly one's seniors wasting energy and good oaths in recounting 'intrigues' against them, and of men who had 'their knife into' their work, or whom they themselves wished to 'knife. ' (This reminded me somehow of the elderly officials who opened their hearts in my old office when they were disappointed over anticipated Honours.) It seemed best to stand clear of it all. For that reason, I have never directly or indirectly criticised any fellow-craftsman's output, or encouraged any man or woman to do so; nor have I approached any persons that they might be led to comment on my output. My acquaintance with my contemporaries has from first to last been very limited.

At 'the little Savile' I remember much kindness and toleration. There was Gosse, of course, sensitive as a cat to all atmospheres, but utterly fearless when it came to questions of good workmanship; Hardy's grave and bitter humour; Andrew Lang, as detached to all appearances as a cloud, but—one learned to know—never kinder in your behalf than when he seemed least concerned with you; Eustace Balfour, a large, lovable man, and one of the best of talkers, who died too soon; Herbert Stephen, very wise and very funny when he chose; Rider Haggard, to whom I took at once, he being of the stamp adored by children and trusted by men at sight; and he could tell tales, mainly against himself, that broke up the tables; Saintsbury, a solid rock of learning and geniality whom I revered all my days;

profoundly a scholar and versed in the art of good living. There was a breakfast with him and Walter Pollock of the Saturday Review in the Albany, when he produced some specially devilish Oriental delicacy which we cooked by the light of our united ignorances. It was splendid! Why those two men took the trouble to notice me, I never knew; but I learned to rely on Saintsbury's judgment in the weightier matters of the Laws of Literature. At his latter end he gave me inestimable help in a little piece of work called 'Proofs of Holy Writ, ' which without his books could never have been handled. I found him at Bath, compiling with erudition equal to his earnestness the Cellar-book of the Queen's Doll's House. He produced a bottle of real Tokay, which I tasted, and lost my number badly by saying that it reminded me of some medicinal wine. It is true he merely called me a blasphemer of the worst, but what he thought I do not care to think!

There were scores of other good men at the Savile, but the tones and the faces of those I have named come back clearest.

My home life—it was a far cry from Piccadilly to Villiers Street—was otherwise, through the months of amazement which followed my return to England. That period was all, as I have said, a dream, in which it seemed that I could push down walls, walk through ramparts and stride across rivers. Yet I was so ignorant, I never guessed when the great fogs fell that trains could take me to light and sunshine a few miles outside London. Once I faced the reflection of my own face in the jet-black mirror of the window-panes for five days. When the fog thinned, I looked out and saw a man standing opposite the pub where the barmaid lived. Of a sudden his breast turned dull red like a robin's, and he crumpled, having cut his throat. In a few minutes—seconds it seemed—a hand-ambulance arrived and took up the body. A pot-boy with a bucket of steaming water sluiced the blood off into the gutter, and what little crowd had collected went its way.

One got to know that ambulance (it lived somewhere at the back of St. Clement Danes) as well as the Police of the E. Division, and even as far as Piccadilly Circus, where, any time after 10.30 P. M., the forces might be found at issue with 'real ladies. ' And through all this shifting, shouting brotheldom the pious British householder and his family bored their way back from the theatres, eyes-front and fixed, as though not seeing.

Among my guests in chambers was a Lion Comique from Gatti's— an artist with sound views on art. According to him, 'it was all right to keep on knockin' 'em' ('puttin' it across' came later) 'but, outside o' that, a man wants something to lay hold of. I'd ha' got it, I think, but for this dam' whisky. But, take it from me, life's all a bloomin' kick-up. ' Certainly my life was; but, to some extent, my Indian training served to ballast me.

I was plentifully assured, viva voce and in the Press-cuttings—which is a drug that I do not recommend to the young—that 'nothing since Dickens' compared with my 'meteoric rise to fame, ' etc. (But I was more or less inoculated, if not immune, to the coarser sorts of print.) And there was my portrait to be painted for the Royal Academy as a notoriety. (But I had a Muhammedan's objection to having my face taken, as likely to draw the Evil Eye. So I was not too puffed up.) And there were letters and letters of all sorts of tendencies. (But if I answered them all I might as well be back at my old table.) And there were proposals from 'certain people of importance, ' insistent and unscrupulous as horse-copers, telling me how 'the ball was at my feet' and that I had only to kick it—by repeating the notes I had already struck and trailing characters I had already 'created' through impossible scenes—to achieve all sorts of desirable things. But I had seen men as well as horses foundered in my lost world behind me. One thing only stood fast through this welter. I was making money—much more than four hundred rupees a month—and when my Bank-book told me I had one thousand whole pounds saved, the Strand was hardly wide enough for my triumph. I had intended a book 'to take advantage of the market. ' This I had just sense enough to countermand. What I most needed was that my people should come over and see what had overtaken their son. This they did on a flying visit, and then my 'kickup' had some worth.

As always, they seemed to suggest nothing and interfere nowhere. But they were there—my Father with his sage Yorkshire outlook and wisdom; my Mother, all Celt and three-parts fire—both so entirely comprehending that except in trivial matters we had hardly need of words.

I think I can with truth say that those two made for me the only public for whom then I had any regard whatever till their deaths, in my forty-fifth year. Their arrival simplified things, and 'set' in my head a notion that had been rising at the back of it. It seemed easy enough to 'knock 'em'—but to what end beyond the heat of the exercise? (That both my grandfathers had been Wesleyan Ministers did not strike me till I was, familiarly, reminded of it.) I had been at work on the rough of a set of verses called later 'The English Flag' and had boggled at a line which had to be a key-line but persisted in going 'soft. ' As was the custom between us, I asked into the air 'What am I trying to get at? ' Instantly the Mother, with her quick flutter of the hands 'You're trying to say; "What do they know of England who only England know, "' The Father confirmed. The rest of the rhetoric came away easily; for it was only pictures seen, as it were, from the deck of a long fourteen-footer, a craft that will almost sail herself.

In the talks that followed, I exposed my notion of trying to tell to the English something of the world outside England—not directly but by implication.

They understood. Long before the end the Mother, summarising, said; 'I see. "Unto them did he discover His swan's nest among the reeds. " Thank you for telling us, dear. ' That settled that; and when Lord Tennyson (whom alas! I never had the good fortune to meet) expressed his approval of the verses when they appeared, I took it for a lucky sign. Most men properly broke to a trade pick up some sort of workshop facility which gives them an advantage over their untrained fellows. My office-work had taught me to think out a notion in detail, pack it away in my head, and work on it by snatches in any surroundings. The lurch and surge of the old horse-drawn buses made a luxurious cradle for such ruminations. Bit by bit, my original notion grew into a vast, vague conspectus—Army and Navy Stores List if you like—of the whole sweep and meaning of things and effort and origins throughout the Empire. I visualised it, as I do most ideas, in the shape of a semi-circle of buildings and temples projecting into a sea-of dreams. At any rate, after I had got it straight in my head, I felt there need be no more 'knockin' 'em' in the abstract.

Likewise, in my wanderings beyond Villiers Street, I had met several men and an occasional woman, whom I by no means loved. They were overly soft-spoken or blatant, and dealt in pernicious varieties of safe sedition. For the most part they seemed to be purveyors of luxuries to the 'Aristocracy, ' whose destruction by painful means they loudly professed to desire. They derided my poor little Gods of the East, and asserted that the British in India spent violent lives 'oppressing' the Native. (This in a land where white girls of sixteen, at twelve or fourteen pounds per annum, hauled thirty and forty pounds weight of bath-water at a time up four flights of stairs!)

The more subtle among them had plans, which they told me, for 'snatching away England's arms when she isn't looking—just like a naughty child—so that when she wants to fight she'll find she can't. ' (We have come far on that road since.) Meantime, their aim was peaceful, intellectual penetration and the formation of what to-day would be called 'cells' in unventilated corners. Collaborating with these gentry was a mixed crowd of wide-minded, wide-mouthed Liberals, who darkened counsel with pious but disintegrating catch-words, and took care to live very well indeed. Somewhere, playing up to them, were various journals, not at all badly written, with a most enviable genius for perverting or mistaking anything that did not suit their bilious doctrine. The general situation, as I saw it, promised an alluring 'dog-fight, ' in which I had no need to take aggressive part because, as soon as the first bloom had faded off my work, my normal output seemed to have the gift of arriding per se the very people I most disliked. And I had the additional luck not to be taken seriously for some time. People talked, quite reasonably, of rockets and sticks; and that genius, J.K. S., brother to Herbert Stephen, dealt with Haggard and me in some stanzas which I would have given much to have written myself. They breathed a prayer for better days when: —

The world shall cease to wonder
    At the genius of an Ass,
And a boy's eccentric blunder
    Shall not bring success to pass:

When there stands a muzzled stripling,
    Mute, beside a muzzled bore
When the Rudyards cease from Kipling
    And the Haggards Ride no more.

It ran joyously through all the papers. It still hangs faintly in the air and, as I used to warn Haggard, may continue as an aroma when all but our two queer names are forgotten.

Several perfectly good reviewers also helped me by demonstrating how I had arrived at my effects by a series of happy accidents. One kind man even went to some trouble, including a good dinner, to discover personally whether I had 'ever read much. ' I could not do less than confirm his worst suspicions, for I had been 'taken on' in that way at the Punjab Club, till my examiner found out that I was pulling his leg, and chased me all round the compound. (The greatest reverence is due to the young. They have, when irritated, little of their own.)

But in all this jam of work done or devising, demands, distractions, excitements, and promiscuous confusions, my health cracked again. I had broken down twice in India from straight overwork, plus fever and dysentery, but this time the staleness and depression came after a bout of real influenza, when all my Indian microbes joined hands and sang for a month in the darkness of Villiers Street.

So I took ship to Italy, and there chanced to meet Lord Dufferin, our Ambassador, who had been Viceroy of India and had known my people. Also, I had written some verses called 'The Song of the Women' about Lady Dufferin's maternity work for women in India, which both she and he liked. He was kindness itself, and made me his guest at his Villa near Naples where, one evening between lights, he talked—at first to me directly, then sliding into a reverie—of his work in India, Canada, and the world at large. I had seen administrative machinery from beneath, all stripped and overheated. This was the first time I had listened to one who had handled it from above. And unlike the generality of Viceroys, Lord Dufferin knew. Of all his revelations and reminiscences, the sentence that stays with me is 'And so, you see, there can be no room' (or was it 'allowance'?) 'for good intentions in one's work. '

Italy, however, was not enough. My need was to get clean away and re-sort myself. Cruises were then unknown; but my dependence was Cook. For the great J. M. himself—the man with the iron mouth and domed brow—had been one of my Father's guests at Lahore when he was trying to induce the Indian Government to let him take over the annual pilgrimage to Mecca as a business proposition. Had he succeeded some lives, and perhaps a war or two, might have been saved. His home offices took friendly interest in my plans and steamer connections.

I sailed first to Cape Town in a gigantic three-thousand-ton liner called The Moor, not knowing I was in the hands of Fate. Aboard her, I met a Navy Captain going to a new Command at Simon's Town. At Madeira he desired to lay in wine for his two-year commission. I assisted him through a variegated day and fluctuating evening, which laid the foundations of life-long friendship.

Cape Town in '91 was a sleepy, unkempt little place, where the stoeps of some of the older Dutch houses still jutted over the pavement. Occasional cows strolled up the main streets, which were full of coloured people of the sort that my ayah had pointed out to me were curly-haired (hubshees) who slept in such posture as made it easy for the devils to enter their bodies. But there were also many Malays who were Muslims of a sort and had their own Mosques, and whose flamboyantly-attired women sold flowers on the kerb, and took in washing. The dry, spiced smell of the land and the smack of the clean sunshine were health-restoring. My Navy Captain introduced me to the Naval society of Simon's Town, where the south-easter blows five days a week, and the Admiral of the Cape Station lived in splendour, with at least a brace of live turtles harnessed to the end of a little wooden jetty, swimming about till due to be taken up for turtle soup. The Navy Club there and the tales of the junior officers delighted me beyond words. There I witnessed one of the most comprehensive 'rags' I had ever seen. It rose out of a polite suggestion to a newly-appointed Lieutenant-Commander that the fore-topmast of his tiny gunboat 'wanted staying forward. ' It went on till all the furniture was completely rearranged all over the room. (How was I to guess that in a few years I should know Simon's Town like the inside of my own pocket, and should give much of my life and love to the glorious land around it?)

We parted, my Captain and I, after a farewell picnic, among white, blowing sand where natives were blasting and where, of a sudden, a wrathful baboon came down the rock-face and halted waistdeep in a bed of arum-lilies. 'We'll meet again, ' said my Captain, 'and if ever you want a cruise, let me know. '

A day or so before my departure for Australia, I lunched at an Adderley Street restaurant next to three men. One of them, I was told, was Cecil Rhodes, who had made the staple of our passengers' talk on The Moor coming out. It never occurred to me to speak to him; and I have often wondered why. . . .

Her name was The Doric. She was almost empty, and she spent twenty-four consecutive days and nights trying, all but successfully, to fill her boats at one roll and empty them down the saloon skylight the next. Sea and sky were equally grey and naked on that weary run to Melbourne. Then I found myself in a new land with new smells and among people who insisted a little too much that they also were new. But there are no such things as new people in this very old world.

The leading paper offered me the most distinguished honour of describing the Melbourne Cup, but I had reported races before and knew it was not in my line. I was more interested in the middle-aged men who had spent their lives making or managing the land. They were direct of speech among each other, and talked a political slang new to me. One learned, as one always does, more from what they said to each other or took for granted in their talk, than one could have got at from a hundred questions. And on a warm night I attended a Labour Congress, where Labour debated whether some much-needed lifeboats should be allowed to be ordered from England, or whether the order should be postponed till life-boats could be built in Australia under Labour direction at Labour prices.

Hereafter my memories of Australian travel are mixed up with trains transferring me, at unholy hours, from one too-exclusive State gauge to another; of enormous skies and primitive refreshment rooms, where I drank hot tea and ate mutton, while now and then a hot wind, like the loo of the Punjab, boomed out of the emptiness. A hard land, it seemed to me, and made harder for themselves by the action of its inhabitants, who—it may have been the climate—always seemed a bit on edge.

I went also to Sydney, which was populated by leisured multitudes all in their shirt-sleeves and all picnicking all the day. They volunteered that they were new and young, but would do wonderful things some day, which promise they more than kept. Then to Hobart, in Tasmania, to pay my respects to Sir George Grey, who had been Governor at Cape Town in the days of the Mutiny. He was very old, very wise and foreseeing, with the gentleness that accompanies a certain sort of strength.

Then came New Zealand by steamer (one was always taking small and rickety coast-wise craft across those big seas), and at Wellington I was met, precisely where warned to expect him, by 'Pelorus Jack, ' the big, white-marked dolphin, who held it his duty to escort shipping up the harbour. He enjoyed a special protection of the Legislature proclaiming him sacred, but, years later, some animal shot and wounded him and he was no more seen. Wellington opened another world of kindly people, more homogeneous, it struck me, than the Australian, large, long-eyelashed, and extraordinarily good-looking. Maybe I was prejudiced, because no less than ten beautiful maidens took me for a row in a big canoe by moonlight on the still waters of Wellington Harbour, and everyone generally put aside everything for my behoof, instruction, amusement, and comfort. So, indeed, it has always been. For which reason I deserve no credit when my work happens to be accurate in detail. A friend long ago taxed me with having enjoyed the 'income of a Prince and the treatment of an Ambassador, ' and with not appreciating it. He even called me, among other things, 'an ungrateful hound. ' But what, I ask you, could I have done except go on with my work and try to add to the pleasure of those that had found it pleasant? One cannot repay the unrepayable by grins and handshakes.

From Wellington I went north towards Auckland in a buggy with a small grey mare, and a most taciturn driver. It was bush country after rain. We crossed a rising river twenty-three times in one day, and came out on great plains where wild horses stared at us, and caught their feet in long blown manes as they stamped and snorted. At one of our halts I was given for dinner a roast bird with a skin like pork crackling, but it had no wings nor trace of any. It was a kiwi—an apteryx. I ought to have saved its skeleton, for few men have eaten apteryx. Hereabouts my driver—I had seen the like happen in lonely places before—exploded, as sometimes solitaries will. We passed a horse's skull beside the track, at which he began to swear horribly but without passion. He had, he said, driven and ridden past that skull for a very long time. To him it meant the lock on the chain of his bondage to circumstance, and why the hell did I come along talking about all those foreign, far places I had seen? Yet he made me go on telling him.

I had had some notion of sailing from Auckland to visit Robert Louis Stevenson at Samoa, for he had done me the honour to write me about some of my tales; and moreover I was Eminent Past Master R. L.S. Even to-day I would back myself to take seventy-five per cent marks in written or viva-voce examination on The Wrong Box which, as the Initiated know, is the Test Volume of that Degree. I read it first in a small hotel in Boston in '89, when the negro waiter nearly turned me out of the dining-room for spluttering over my meal.

But Auckland, soft and lovely in the sunshine, seemed the end of organised travel; for the captain of a fruit-boat, which might or might not go to Samoa at some time or other, was so devotedly drunk that I decided to turn south, and work back to India. All I carried away from the magic town of Auckland was the face and voice of a woman who sold me beer at a little hotel there. They stayed at the back of my head till ten years later when, in a local train of the Cape Town suburbs, I heard a petty officer from Simon's Town telling a companion about a woman in New Zealand who 'never scrupled to help a lame duck or put her foot on a scorpion. ' Then—precisely as the removal of the key-log in a timber jam starts the whole pile—those words gave me the key to the face and voice at Auckland, and a tale called 'Mrs. Bathurst' slid into my mind, smoothly and orderly as floating timber on a bank-high river.

The South Island, mainly populated by Scots, their sheep, and the Devil's own high winds, I tackled in another small steamer, among colder and increasing seas. We cleared it at the Last Lamp-post in the World—Invercargill—on a boisterous dark evening, when General Booth of the Salvation Army came on board. I saw him walking backward in the dusk over the uneven wharf, his cloak blown upwards, tulip-fashion, over his grey head, while he beat a tambourine in the face of the singing, weeping, praying crowd who had come to see him off.

We stood out, and at once took the South Pacific. For the better part of a week we were swept from end to end, our poop was split, and a foot or two of water smashed through the tiny saloon. I remember no set meals. The General's cabin was near mine, and in the intervals between crashes overhead and cataracts down below he sounded like a wounded elephant; for he was in every way a big man.

I saw no more of him till I had picked up my P. &0., which also happened to be his, for Colombo at Adelaide. Here all the world came out in paddle-boats and small craft to speed him on his road to

India. He spoke to them from our upper deck, and one of his gestures—an imperative, repeated, downward sweep of the arm—puzzled me, till I saw that a woman crouching on the paddle-box of a crowded boat had rucked her petticoats well up to her knees. In those days righteous woman ended at the neck and instep. Presently, she saw what was troubling the General. Her skirts were adjusted and all was peace and piety. I talked much with General Booth during that voyage. Like the young ass I was, I expressed my distaste at his appearance on Invercargill wharf. 'Young feller, ' he replied, bending great brows at me, 'if I thought I could win one more soul to the Lord by walking on my head and playing the tambourine with my toes, I'd—I'd learn how. '

He had the right of it ('if by any means I can save some') and I had decency enough to apologise. He told me about the beginnings of his mission, and how surely he would be in gaol were his accounts submitted to any sort of official inspection; and how his work must be a one-man despotism with only the Lord for supervisor. (Even so spoke Paul and, I am well sure, Muhammed.)

'Then why, ' I asked, 'can't you stop your Salvation lasses from going out to India and living alone native-fashion among natives? ' I told him something of village conditions in India. The despot's defence was very human. 'But what am I to do? ' he demanded. 'The girls will go, and one can't stop 'em. '

I think this first flare of enthusiasm was rationalised later, but not before some good lives had been expended. I conceived great respect and admiration for this man with the head of Isaiah and the fire of the Prophet, but, like the latter, rather at sea among women. The next time I met him was at Oxford when Degrees were being conferred. He strode across to me in his Doctor's robes, which magnificently became him, and, 'Young feller, ' said he, 'how's your soul? '

I have always liked the Salvation Army, of whose work outside England I have seen a little. They are, of course, open to all the objections urged against them by science and the regular creeds; but it seems to me that when a soul conceives itself as being reborn it may go through agonies both unscientific and unregulated. Haggard, who had worked with him and for the Army on several occasions, told me that for sheer luxury of attendance, kindliness, and good-will, nothing compared with travel under their care.

From Colombo I crossed over to the India of the extreme south which I did not know, and for four days and four nights in the belly of the train could not understand one word of the speech around me. Then came the open north and Lahore, where I was snatching a few days' visit with my people. They were coming 'Home' for good soon; so this was my last look round the only real home I had yet known.

Chapter V

The Committee of Ways and Means

Then down to Bombay where my ayah, so old but so unaltered, met me with blessings and tears; and then to London to be married in January '92 in the thick of an influenza epidemic, when the undertakers had run out of black horses and the dead had to be content with brown ones. The living were mostly abed. (We did not know then that this epidemic was the first warning that the plague—forgotten for generations—was on the move out of Manchuria.)

All of which touched me as much as it would any other young man under like circumstances. My concern was to get out of the pest-house as soon as might be. For was I not a person of substance? Had I not several—more than two at least—thousand pounds in Fixed Deposits? Had not my own Bank's Manager himself suggested that I might invest some of my 'capital' in, say, indigo? But I preferred to invest once more in Cook's tickets—for two—on a voyage round the world. It was all arranged beyond any chance of failure.

So we were married in the church with the pencil-pointed steeple at Langham Place—Gosse, Henry James, and my cousin Ambrose Poynter being all the congregation present—and we parted at the church door to the scandal of the Beadle, my wife to administer medicine to her mother, and I to a wedding breakfast with Ambrose Poynter; after which, on returning to collect my wife, I saw, pinned down by weights on the rainy pavement as was the custom of those untroubled days, a newspaper poster announcing my marriage, which made me feel uncomfortable and defenceless.

And a few days afterwards we were on our magic carpet which was to take us round the earth, beginning with Canada deep in snow. Among our wedding gifts was a generous silver flask filled with whisky, but of incontinent habit. It leaked in the valise where it lay with flannel shirts. And it scented the entire Pullman from end to end ere we arrived at the cause. But by that time all our fellow-passengers were pitying that poor girl who had linked her life to this shameless inebriate. Thus in a false atmosphere all of our innocent own, we came to Vancouver, where with an eye to the future and for proof of wealth we bought, or thought we had, twenty acres of a wilderness called North Vancouver, now part of the City. But there was a catch in the thing, as we found many years later when, after paying taxes on it for ever so long, we discovered it belonged to some one else. All the consolation we got then from the smiling people of Vancouver was; 'You bought that from Steve, did you? Ah-ah, Steve! You hadn't ought to ha' bought from Steve. No! Not from Steve. ' And thus did, the good Steve cure us of speculating in real estate.

Then to Yokohama, where we were treated with all the kindliness in the world by a man and his wife on whom we had no shadow of any claim. They made us more than welcome in their house, and saw to it that we should see Japan in wistaria and peony time. Here an earthquake (prophetic as it turned out) overtook us one hot break of dawn, and we fled out into the garden, where a tall cryptomeria waggled its insane head back and forth with an 'I told you so' expression; though not a breath was stirring. A little later I went to the Yokohama branch of my Bank on a wet forenoon to draw some of my solid wealth. Said the Manager to me: 'Why not take more? It will be just as easy. ' I answered that I did not care to have too much cash at one time in my careless keeping, but that when I had looked over my accounts I might come again in the afternoon. I did so; but in that little space my Bank, the notice on its shut door explained, had suspended payment. (Yes, I should have done better to have invested my 'capital' as its London Manager had hinted.)

I returned with my news to my bride of three months and a child to be born. Except for what I had drawn that morning—the Manager had sailed as near to the wind as loyalty permitted—and the unexpended Cook vouchers, and our personal possessions in our trunks, we had nothing whatever. There was an instant Committee of Ways and Means, which advanced our understanding of each other more than a cycle of solvent matrimony. Retreat—flight, if you like—was indicated. What would Cook return for the tickets, not including the price of lost dreams? 'Every pound you've paid, of course, ' said Cook of Yokohama. 'These things are all luck and— here's your refund. '

Back again, then, across the cold North Pacific, through Canada on the heels of the melting snows, and to the outskirts of a little New England town where my wife's paternal grandfather (a French man) had made his home and estate many years before. The country was large-boned, mountainous, wooded, and divided into farms of from fifty to two hundred barren acres. Roads, sketched in dirt, connected white, clap-boarded farm-houses, where the older members of the families made shift to hold down the eating mortgages. The younger folk had gone elsewhere. There were many abandoned houses too; some decaying where they stood; others already reduced to a stone chimney-stack or mere green dimples still held by an undefeated lilac-bush. On one small farm was a building known as the Bliss Cottage, generally inhabited by a hired man. It was of one storey and a half; seventeen feet high to the roof-tree; seventeen feet deep and, including the kitchen and wood-shed, twenty-seven feet wide over all. Its water-supply was a single half-inch lead pipe connecting with a spring in the neighbourhood. But it was habitable, and it stood over a deep if dampish cellar. Its rent was ten dollars or two pounds a month.

We took it. We furnished it with a simplicity that fore-ran the hire-purchase system. We bought, second or third hand, a huge, hot-air stove which we installed in the cellar. We cut generous holes in our thin floors for its eightinch tin pipes (why we were not burned in our beds each week of the winter I never can understand) and we were extraordinarily and self-centredly content.

As the New England summer flamed into autumn I piled cut spruce boughs all round the draughty cottage sill, and helped to put up a tiny roofless verandah along one side of it for future needs. When winter shut down and sleigh-bells rang all over the white world that tucked us in, we counted ourselves secure. Sometimes we had a servant. Sometimes she would find the solitude too much for her and flee without warning, one even leaving her trunk. This troubled us not at all. There are always two sides to a plate, and the cleaning of frying- and saucepans is as little a mystery as the making of comfortable beds. When our lead pipe froze, we would slip on our coon-skin coats and thaw it out with a lighted candle. There was no space in the attic bedroom for a cradle, so we decided that a trunk-tray would be just as good. We envied no one—not even when skunks wandered into our cellar and, knowing the nature of the beasts, we immobilised ourselves till it should please them to depart.

But our neighbours saw no humour in our proceedings. Here was a stranger of an unloved race, currently reported to 'make as much as a hundred dollars out of a ten-cent bottle of ink, ' and who had 'pieces in the papers' about him, who had married a 'Balestier girl. ' Did not her grandmother still live on the Balestier place, where 'old Balestier' instead of farming had built a large house, and there had dined late in special raiment, and drunk red wines after the custom of the French instead of decent whisky? And behold this Britisher, under pretext of having lost money, had settled his wife down 'right among her own folk' in the Bliss Cottage. It was not seemly on the face of it; so they watched as secretively as the New England or English peasant can, and what toleration they extended to the 'Britisher' was solely for the sake of 'the Balestier girl. '

But we had received the first shock of our young lives at the first crisis in them. The Committee of Ways and Means passed a resolution, never rescinded, that henceforth, at any price, it must own its collective self.

As money came in from the sale of books and tales, the first use we made of it was to buy back Departmental Ditties, Plain Tales, and the six paperbacked books that I had sold to get me funds for leaving India in '89. They cost something, but, owning them, the Bliss Cottage breathed more comfortably.

Not till much later did we realise the terrible things that 'folks thought of your doin's. ' From their point of view they were right. Also, they were practical as the following will show.

One day a stranger drove up to the Bliss Cottage. The palaver opened thus: —

'Kiplin', ain't ye? '

That was admitted.

'Write, don't ye? '

That seemed accurate. (Long pause.)

'Thet bein' so, you've got to live to please folk, hain't ye? '

That indeed was the raw truth. He sat rigid in the buggy and went on.

'Thet bein' so, you've got to please to live, I reckon? '

It was true. (I thought of my Adjutant of Volunteers at Lahore.)

'Puttin' it thet way, ' he pursued, 'we'll 'low thet, by and by, ye can't please. Sickness—accident—any darn thing. Then—what's liable to happen ye—both of ye? '

I began to see, and he to fumble in his breast pocket.

'Thet's where Life Insurance comes in. Naow, I represent, ' etc. etc. It was beautiful salesmanship. The Company was reputable, and I effected my first American Insurance, Leuconoë agreeing with Horace to trust the future as little as possible.

Other visitors were not so tactful. Reporters came from papers in Boston, which I presume believed itself to be civilised, and demanded interviews. I told them I had nothing to say. 'If ye hevn't, guess we'll make ye say something. ' So they went away and lied copiously, their orders being to 'get the story. ' This was new to me at the time; but the Press had not got into its full free stride of later years.

My workroom in the Bliss Cottage was seven feet by eight, and from December to April the snow lay level with its window-sill. It chanced that I had written a tale about Indian Forestry work which included a boy who had been brought up by wolves. In the stillness, and suspense, of the winter of '92 some memory of the Masonic Lions of my childhood's magazine, and a phrase in Haggard's Nada the Lily, combined with the echo of this tale. After blocking out the main idea in my head, the pen took charge, and I watched it begin to write stories about Mowgli and animals, which later grew into the Jungle Books.

Once launched there seemed no particular reason to stop, but I had learned to distinguish between the peremptory motions of my Daemon, and the 'carry-over' or induced electricity, which comes of what you might call mere 'frictional' writing. Two tales, I remember, I threw away and was better pleased with the remainder. More to the point, my Father thought well of the workmanship.

My first child and daughter was born in three foot of snow on the night of December 29th, 1892. Her Mother's birthday being the 31st and mine the 30th of the same month, we congratulated her on her sense of the fitness of things, and she throve in her trunk-tray in the sunshine on the little plank verandah. Her birth brought me into contact with the best friend I made in New England—Dr. Conland.
It seemed that the Bliss Cottage might be getting a little congested, so, in the following spring, the Committee of Ways and Means 'considered a field and bought it'—as much as ten whole acres—on a rocky hillside looking across a huge valley to Wantastiquet, the wooded mountain across the Connecticut river.

That summer there came out of Quebec Jean Pigeon with nine other habitants who put up a wooden shed for their own accommodation in what seemed twenty minutes, and then set to work to build us a house which we called 'Naulakha. ' Ninety feet was the length of it and thirty the width, on a high foundation of solid mortared rocks which gave us an airy and a skunk-proof basement. The rest was wood, shingled, roof and sides, with dull green hand-split shingles, and the windows were lavish and wide. Lavish too was the long open attic, as I realised when too late. Pigeon asked me whether I would have it finished in ash or cherry. Ignorant that I was, I chose ash, and so missed a stretch of perhaps the most satisfying interior wood that is grown. Those were opulent days, when timber was nothing regarded, and the best of cabinet-work could be had for little money.

Next, we laid out a long drive to the road. This needed dynamite to soften its grades and a most mellow plumber brought up many sticks of it all rattling about under his buggy-seat among the tamping-rods. We dived, like woodchucks, into the nearest deepest hole. Next, needing water, we sunk a five-inch shaft three hundred foot into the New England granite, which nowhere was less than three, though some say thirty, thousand foot thick. Over that we set a windmill, which gave us not enough water and moaned and squeaked o' nights. So we knocked out its lowest bolts, hitched on two yoke of bullocks, and overthrew it, as it might have been the Vend'me Column; thus spiritually recouping ourselves for at least half the cost of erection. A low-power atmospheric pump, which it was my disgustful duty to oil, was its successor. These experiences gave us both a life-long taste for playing with timber, stone, concrete and such delightful things.

Horses were an integral part of our lives, for the Bliss Cottage was three miles from the little town, and half a mile from the house in building. Our permanent servitor was a big, philosophical black called Marcus Aurelius, who waited in the buggy as cars wait to-day, and when weary of standing up would carefully lie down and go to sleep between his shafts. After we had finished with him, we tied his reins short and sent him in charge of the buggy alone down the road to his stable-door, where he resumed his slumbers till some one came to undress him and put him to bed. There was a small mob of other horses about the landscape, including a meek old stallion with a permanently lame leg, who passed the evening of his days in a horse-power machine which cut wood for us.

I tried to give something of the fun and flavour of those days in a story called 'A Walking Delegate' where all the characters are from horse-life.

The wife's passion, I discovered, was driving trotters. It chanced that our first winter in 'Naulakha' she went to look at the new patent safety heating-stove, which blew flame in her face and burnt it severely. She recovered slowly, and Dr. Conland suggested that she needed a tonic. I had been in treaty for a couple of young, sealbrown, full brother and sister Morgans, good for a three-mile clip, and, on Conland's hint, concluded the deal. When I told the wife, she thought it would console her to try them and, that same afternoon, leaving one eye free of the bandages, she did so in three foot of snow and a failing light, while I suffered beside her. But Nip and Tuck were perfect roadsters and the 'tonic' succeeded. After that they took us all over the large countryside.

It would be hard to exaggerate the loneliness and sterility of life on the farms. The land was denuding itself of its accustomed inhabitants, and their places had not yet been taken by the wreckage of Eastern Europe or the wealthy city folk who later bought 'pleasure farms. ' What might have become characters, powers and attributes perverted themselves in that desolation as cankered trees throw out branches akimbo, and strange faiths and cruelties, born of solitude to the edge of insanity, flourished like lichen on sick bark.

One day-long excursion up the flanks of Wantastiquet, our guardian mountain across the river, brought us to a farm-house where we were welcomed by the usual wild-eyed, flat-fronted woman of the place. Looking over sweeps of emptiness, we saw our 'Naulakha' riding on its hillside like a little boat on the flank of a far wave. Said the woman, fiercely; 'Be you the new lights 'crost the valley yonder? Ye don't know what a comfort they've been to me this winter. Ye aren't ever goin' to shroud 'em up—or be ye? ' So, as long as we lived there, that broad side of 'Naulakha' which looked her-ward was always nakedly lit.
In the little town where we shopped there was another atmosphere. Vermont was by tradition a 'Dry' State. For that reason, one found in

almost every office the water-bottle and thick tooth-glass displayed openly, and in discreet cupboards or drawers the whisky bottle. Business was conducted and concluded with gulps of raw spirit, followed by a pledget of ice-cold water. Then, both parties chewed cloves, but whether to defeat the Law, which no one ever regarded, or to deceive their women-folk, of whom they went in great fear (they were mostly educated up to College age by spinsters), I do not know.

But a promising scheme for a Country Club had to be abandoned because many men who would by right belong to it could not be trusted with a full whisky bottle. On the farms, of course, men drank cider, of various strengths, and sometimes achieved almost maniacal forms of drunkenness. The whole business seemed to me as unwholesomely furtive and false as many aspects of American life at that time.

Administratively, there was unlimited and meticulous legality, with a multiplication of semi-judicial offices and titles; but of law-abidingness, or of any conception of what that implied, not a trace. Very little in business, transportation, or distribution, that I had to deal with, was sure, punctual, accurate, or organised. But this they neither knew nor would have believed though angels affirmed it. Ethnologically, immigrants were coming into the States at about a million head a year. They supplied the cheap—almost slave—labour, lacking which all wheels would have stopped, and they were handled with a callousness that horrified me. The Irish had passed out of the market into 'politics' which suited their instincts of secrecy, plunder, and anonymous denunciation. The Italians were still at work, laying down trams, but were moving up, via small shops and curious activities, to the dominant position which they now occupy in well-organised society. The German, who had preceded even the Irish, counted himself a full-blooded American, and looked down gutturally on what he called 'foreign trash. ' Somewhere in the background, though he did not know it, was the 'representative' American, who traced his blood through three or four generations and who, controlling nothing and affecting less, protested that the accepted lawlessness of life was not 'representative' of his country, whose moral, aesthetic, and literary champion he had appointed himself. He said too, almost automatically, that all foreign elements could and would soon be 'assimilated' into 'good Americans. ' And not a soul cared what he said or how he said it! They were making or losing money.

The political background of the land was monotonous. When the people looked, which was seldom, outside their own borders, England was still the dark and dreadful enemy to be feared and guarded against. The Irish, whose other creed is Hate; the history books in the Schools; the Orators; the eminent Senators; and above all the Press; saw to that. Now John Hay, one of the very few American Ambassadors to England with two sides to their heads, had his summer house a few hours north by rail from us. On a visit to him, we discussed the matter. His explanation was convincing. I quote the words which stayed textually in my memory. 'America's hatred of England is the hoop round the forty-four (as they were then) staves of the Union. ' He said it was the only standard possible to apply to an enormously variegated population. 'So—when a man comes up out of the sea, we say to him; "See that big bully over there in the East? He's England! Hate him, and you're a good American. "'

On the principle, 'if you can't keep a love affair going, start a row, ' this is reasonable. At any rate the belief lifted on occasion the overwhelming vacuity of the national life into some contact with imponderable externals.

But how thoroughly the doctrine was exploited I did not realise till we visited Washington in '95, where I met Theodore Roosevelt, then Under-Secretary (I never caught the name of the Upper) to the U. S. Navy. I liked him from the first and largely believed in him. He would come to our hotel, and thank God in a loud voice that he had not one drop of British blood in him; his ancestry being Dutch, and his creed conforming-Dopper, I think it is called. Naturally I told him nice tales about his Uncles and Aunts in South Africa—only I called them Ooms and Tanties—who esteemed themselves the sole lawful Dutch under the canopy and dismissed Roosevelt's stock for 'Verdomder Hollanders. ' Then he became really eloquent, and we would go off to the Zoo together, where he talked about grizzlies that he had met. It was laid on him, at that time, to furnish his land with an adequate Navy; the existing collection of unrelated types and casual purchases being worn out. I asked him how he proposed to get it, for the American people did not love taxation. 'Out of you, ' was the disarming reply. And so—to some extent—it was. The obedient and instructed Press explained how England—treacherous and jealous as ever—only waited round the corner to descend on the unprotected coasts of Liberty, and to that end was preparing, etc. etc. etc. (This in '95 when England had more than enough hay on her own trident to keep her busy!) But the trick worked, and all the Orators and Senators gave tongue, like the Hannibal Chollops that they were. I remember the wife of a Senator who, apart from his politics, was very largely civilised, invited me to drop into the Senate and listen to her spouse 'twisting the Lion's tail. ' It seemed an odd sort of refreshment to offer a visitor. I could not go, but I read his speech. [At the present time (autumn '35) I have also read with interest the apology offered by an American Secretary of State to Nazi Germany for unfavourable comments on that land by a New York Police Court Judge.] But those were great and spacious and friendly days in Washington which—politics apart—Allah had not altogether deprived of a sense of humour; and the food was a thing to dream of.

Through Roosevelt I met Professor Langley of the Smithsonian, an old man who had designed a model aeroplane driven—for petrol had not yet arrived—by a miniature flash-boiler engine, a marvel of delicate craftsmanship. It flew on trial over two hundred yards, and drowned itself in the waters of the Potomac, which was cause of great mirth and humour to the Press of his country. Langley took it coolly enough and said to me that, though he would never live till then, I should see the aeroplane established.

The Smithsonian, specially on the ethnological side, was a pleasant place to browse in. Every nation, like every individual, walks in a vain show—else it could not live with itself—but I never got over the wonder of a people who, having extirpated the aboriginals of their continent more completely than any modern race had ever done, honestly believed that they were a godly little New England community, setting examples to brutal mankind. This wonder I used to explain to Theodore Roosevelt, who made the glass cases of Indian relics shake with his rebuttals.

The next time I met him was in England, not long after his country had acquired the Philippines, and he—like an elderly lady with one babe—yearned to advise England on colonial administration. His views were sound enough, for his subject was Egypt as it was beginning to be then, and his text 'Govern or get out. ' He consulted several people as to how far he could go. I assured him that the English would take anything from him, but were racially immune to advice.

I never met him again, but we corresponded through the years when he 'jumped' Panama from a brother-President there whom he described as 'Pithecanthropoid, ' and also during the War, in the course of which I met two of his delightful sons. My own idea of him was that he was a much bigger man than his people understood or, at that time, knew how to use, and that he and they might have been better off had he been born twenty years later.

Meantime, our lives went on at the Bliss Cottage and, so soon as it was built, at 'Naulakha. ' To the former one day came Sam McClure, credited with being the original of Stevenson's Pinkerton in The Wrecker, but himself, far more original. He had been everything from a pedlar to a tintype photographer along the highways, and had held intact his genius and simplicity. He entered, alight with the notion for a new Magazine to be called 'McClure's. ' I think the talk lasted some twelve—or it may have been seventeen—hours, before the notion was fully hatched out. He, like Roosevelt, was in advance of his age, for he looked rather straightly at practices and impostures which were in the course of being sanctified because they paid. People called it 'muck-raking' at the time, and it seemed to do no sort of good. I liked and admired McClure more than a little, for he was one of the few with whom three and a half words serve for a sentence, and as clean and straight as spring water. Nor did I like him less when he made a sporting offer to take all my output for the next few years at what looked like fancy rates. But the Committee of

Ways and Means decided that futures were not to be dealt in. (I here earnestly commend to the attention of the ambitious young a text in the thirty-third chapter of Ecclesiasticus which runs; 'As long as thou livest and hast breath in thee, give not thyself over to any. ')

To 'Naulakha, ' on a wet day, came from Scribner's of New York a large young man called Frank Doubleday, with a proposal, among other things, for a complete edition of my then works. One accepts or refuses things that really matter on personal and illogical grounds. We took to that young man at sight, and he and his wife became of our closest friends. In due time, when he was building up what turned into the great firm of Doubleday, Page & Co., and later Doubleday, Doran & Co., I handed over the American side of my business to him. Whereby I escaped many distractions for the rest of my life. Thanks to the large and intended gaps in the American Copyright law, much could be done by the enterprising not only to steal, which was natural, but to add to and interpolate and embellish the thefts with stuff I had never written. At first this annoyed me, but later I laughed; and Frank Doubleday chased the pirates up with cheaper and cheaper editions, so that their thefts became less profitable. There was no more pretence to morality in these gentlemen than in their brethren, the bootleggers of later years. As a pillar of the Copyright League (even he could not see the humour of it) once said, when I tried to bring him to book for a more than usually flagrant trespass 'We thought there was money in it, so we did it. ' It was, you see, his religion. By and large I should say that American pirates have made say half as many dollars out of my stuff as I am occasionally charged with having 'made' out of the legitimate market in that country.

Into this queer life the Father came to see how we fared, and we two went wandering into Quebec where, the temperature being 95 and all the world dressed all over after the convention of those days, the Father was much amazed. Then we visited at Boston his old friend, Charles Eliot Norton of Harvard, whose daughters I had known at The Grange in my boyhood and since. They were Brahmins of the Boston Brahmins, living delightfully, but Norton himself, full of forebodings as to the future of his land's soul, felt the established earth sliding under him, as horses feel coming earth-tremors.

He told us a tale of old days in New England. He and another Professor, wandering round the country in a buggy and discussing high and moral matters, halted at the farm of an elderly farmer well known to them, who, in the usual silence of New England; set about getting the horse a bucket of water. The two men in the buggy went on with their discussion, in the course of which one of them said; 'Well, according to Montaigne, ' and gave a quotation. Voice from the horse's head, where the farmer was holding the bucket "Tweren't Montaigne said that. 'Twere Mon-tes-ki-ew. ' And 'twas.

That, said Norton, was in the middle or late 'seventies. We two wandered about the back of Shady Hill in a buggy, but nothing of that amazing kind befell us. And Norton spoke of Emerson and Wendell Holmes and Longfellow and the Alcotts and other influences of the past as we returned to his library, and he browsed aloud among his books; for he was a scholar among scholars.

But what struck me, and he owned to something of the same feeling, was the apparent waste and ineffectiveness, in the face of the foreign inrush, of all the indigenous effort of the past generation. It was then that I first began to wonder whether Abraham Lincoln had not killed rather too many autochthonous 'Americans' in the Civil War, for the benefit of their hastily imported Continental supplanters. This is black heresy, but I have since met men and women who have breathed it. The weakest of the old-type immigrants had been sifted and salted by the long sailing-voyage of those days. But steam began in the later 'sixties and early 'seventies, when human cargoes could be delivered with all their imperfections and infections in a fortnight or so. And one million more-or-less acclimatised Americans had been killed.

Somehow or other, between '92 and '96 we managed to pay two flying visits to England, where my people were retired and lived in Wiltshire; and we learned to loathe the cold North Atlantic more and more. On one trip our steamer came almost atop of a whale, who submerged just in time to clear us, and looked up into my face with an unforgettable little eye the size of a bullock's. Eminent Masters R. L.S. will remember what William Dent Pitman saw of 'haughty and indefinable' in the hairdresser's waxen model. When I was illustrating the Just So Stories, I remembered and strove after that eye.

We went once or twice to Gloucester, Mass., on a summer visit, when I attended the annual Memorial Service to the men drowned or lost in the cod-fishing schooners fleet. Gloucester was then the metropolis of that industry.

Now our Dr. Conland had served in that fleet when he was young. One thing leading to another, as happens in this world, I embarked on a little book which was called Captains Courageous. My part was the writing; his the details. This book took us (he rejoicing to escape from the dread respectability of our little town) to the shore-front, and the old T-wharf of Boston Harbour, and to queer meals in sailors' eating-houses, where he renewed his youth among ex-shipmates or their kin. We assisted hospitable tug-masters to help haul three- and four-stick schooners of Pocahontas coal all round the harbour; we boarded every craft that looked as if she might be useful, and we delighted ourselves to the limit of delight. Charts we got—old and new—and the crude implements of navigation such as they used off the Banks, and a battered boat-compass, still a treasure with me. (Also, by pure luck, I had sight of the first sickening uprush and vomit of iridescent coal-dusted water into the hold of a ship, a crippled iron hulk, sinking at her moorings.) And Conland took large cod and the appropriate knives with which they are prepared for the hold, and demonstrated anatomically and surgically so that I could make no mistake about treating them in print. Old tales, too, he dug up, and the lists of dead and gone schooners whom he had loved, and I revelled in profligate abundance of detail—not necessarily for publication but for the joy of it. And he sent me—may he be forgiven! —out on a pollock-fisher, which is ten times fouler than any cod-schooner, and I was immortally sick, even though they tried to revive me with a fragment of unfresh pollock.

As though this were not enough, when, at the end of my tale, I desired that some of my characters should pass from San Francisco to New York in record time, and wrote to a railway magnate of my acquaintance asking what he himself would do, that most excellent man sent a fully worked-out time-table, with watering halts, changes of engine, mileage, track conditions and climates, so that a corpse could not have gone wrong in the schedule. My characters arrived triumphantly; and, then, a real live railway magnate was so moved after reading the book that he called out his engines and called out his men, hitched up his own private car, and set himself to beat my time on paper over the identical route, and succeeded. Yet the book was not all reporterage. I wanted to see if I could catch and hold something of a rather beautiful localised American atmosphere that was already beginning to fade. Thanks to Conland I came near this.

A million—or it may have been only forty—years later, a Super-film Magnate was in treaty with me for the film rights of this book. At the end of the sitting, my Daemon led me to ask if it were proposed to introduce much 'sex appeal' into the great work. 'Why, certainly, ' said he. Now a happily married lady cod-fish lays about three million eggs at one confinement. I told him as much. He said; 'Is that so? ' And went on about 'ideals. '. .. Conland had been long since dead, but I prayed that wherever he was, he might have heard.

And so, in this unreal life, indoors and out, four years passed, and a good deal of verse and prose saw the light. Better than all, I had known a corner of the United States as a householder, which is the only way of getting at a country. Tourists may carry away impressions, but it is the seasonal detail of small things and doings (such as putting up fly-screens and stove-pipes, buying yeast-cakes and being lectured by your neighbours) that bite in the lines of mental pictures. They were an interesting folk, but behind their desperate activities lay always, it seemed to me, immense and unacknowledged boredom—the deadweight of material things passionately worked up into Gods, that only bored their worshippers more and worse and longer. The intellectual influences of their Continental immigrants were to come later. At this time they were still more or less connected with the English tradition and schools, and the Semitic strain had not yet been uplifted in a too-much-at-ease Zion. So far as I was concerned, I felt the atmosphere was to some extent hostile. The idea seemed to be that I was 'making money' out of America—witness the new house and the horses—and was not sufficiently grateful for my privileges. My visits to England and the talk there persuaded me that the English scene might be shifting to some new developments, which would be worth watching. A meeting of the Committee of Ways and Means came to the conclusion that 'Naulakha, ' desirable as it was, meant only 'a house' and not 'The House' of our dreams. So we loosed hold and, with another small daughter, born in the early spring snows and beautifully tanned in a sumptuous upper verandah, we took ship for England, after clearing up all our accounts. As Emerson wrote: —

Wilt thou seal up the avenues of ill?
Pay every debt as if God wrote the bill.

The spring of '96 saw us in Torquay, where we found a house for our heads that seemed almost too good to be true. It was large and bright, with big rooms each and all open to the sun, the grounds embellished with great trees and the warm land dipping southerly to the clean sea under the Marychurch cliffs. It had been inhabited for thirty years by three old maids. We took it hopefully. Then we made two notable discoveries. Everybody was learning to ride things called 'bicycles. ' In Torquay there was a circular cinder-track where, at stated hours, men and women rode solemnly round and round on them. Tailors supplied special costumes for this sport. Some one—I think it was Sam McClure from America—had given us a tandem bicycle, whose double steering-bars made good dependence for continuous domestic quarrel. On this devil's toast-rack we took exercise, each believing that the other liked it. We even rode it through the idle, empty lanes, and would pass or overtake without upset several carts in several hours. But, one fortunate day, it skidded, and decanted us on to the roadmetal. Almost before we had risen from our knees, we made mutual confession of our common loathing of wheels, pushed the Hell-Spider home by hand, and rode it no more.

The other revelation came in the shape of a growing depression which enveloped us both—a gathering blackness of mind and sorrow of the heart, that each put down to the new, soft climate and, without telling the other, fought against for long weeks. It was the Feng-shui—the Spirit of the house itself—that darkened the sunshine and fell upon us every time we entered, checking the very words on our lips.

A talk about a doubtful cistern brought another mutual confession. 'But I thought you liked the place? ' 'But I made sure you did, ' was the burden of our litanies. Using the cistern for a stalking-horse, we paid forfeit and fled. More than thirty years later on a motor-trip we ventured down the steep little road to that house, and met, almost unchanged, the gardener and his wife in the large, open, sunny stable-yard, and, quite unchanged, the same brooding Spirit of deep, deep Despondency within the open, lit rooms.

But while we were at Torquay there came to me the idea of beginning some tracts or parables on the education of the young. These, for reasons honestly beyond my control, turned themselves into a series of tales called Stalky & Co. My very dear Headmaster, Cormell Price, who had now turned into 'Uncle Crom' or just 'Crommy, ' paid a visit at the time and we discussed school things generally. He said, with the chuckle that I had reason to know, that my tracts would be some time before they came to their own. On their appearance they were regarded as irreverent, not true to life, and rather 'brutal. ' This led me to wonder, not for the first time, at which end of their carcasses grown men keep their school memories.

Talking things over with 'Crommy, ' I reviled him for the badness and scantiness of our food at Westward Ho! To which he replied; 'We-el! For one thing, we were all as poor as church mice. Can you remember any one who had as much as a bob a week pocket money? I can't. For an other, a boy who is always hungry is more interested in his belly than in anything else. ' (In the Boer War I learned that the virtue in a battalion living on what is known as 'Two and a half'— Army biscuits—a day is severe.) Speaking of sickness and epidemics, which were unknown to us, he said; 'I expect you were healthy because you lived in the open almost as much as Dartmoor ponies. ' Stalky & Co. became the illegitimate ancestor of several stories of school-life whose heroes lived through experiences mercifully denied to me. It is still read ('35) and I maintain it is a truly valuable collection of tracts.

Our flight from Torquay ended almost by instinct at Rottingdean where the beloved Aunt and Uncle had their holiday house, and where I had spent my very last days before sailing for India fourteen years back. In 1882 there had been but one daily bus from Brighton, which took forty minutes; and when a stranger appeared on the village green the native young would stick out their tongues at him. The Downs poured almost direct into the one village street and lay out eastward unbroken to Russia Hill above Newhaven. It was little altered in '96. My cousin, Stanley Baldwin, had married the eldest daughter of the Ridsdales out of The Dene—the big house that flanked one side of the green. My Uncle's 'North End House' commanded the other, and a third house opposite the church was waiting to be taken according to the decrees of Fate. The Baldwin marriage, then, made us free of the joyous young brotherhood and sisterhood of The Dene, and its friends.

The Aunt and the Uncle had said to us; 'Let the child that is coming to you be born in our house, ' and had effaced themselves till my son John arrived on a warm August night of '97, under what seemed every good omen. Meantime, we had rented by direct interposition of Fate that third house opposite the church on the green. It stood in a sort of little island behind flint walls which we then thought were high enough, and almost beneath some big ilex trees. It was small, none too well built, but cheap, and so suited us who still remembered a little affair at Yokohama. Then there grew up great happiness between 'The Dene, ' 'North End House, ' and 'The Elms. ' One could throw a cricket-ball from any one house to the other, but, beyond turning out at 2 A. M. to help a silly foxhound puppy who had stuck in a drain, I do not remember any violent alarms and excursions other than packing farmcarts filled with mixed babies— Stanley Baldwin's and ours—and despatching them into the safe clean heart of the motherly Downs for jam-smeared picnics. Those

Downs moved me to write some verses called 'Sussex. ' To-day, from Rottingdean to Newhaven is almost fully developed suburb, of great horror.

When the Burne-Jones' returned to their own 'North End House, ' all was more than well. My Uncle's world was naturally not mine, but his heart and brain were large enough to take in any universe, and in the matter of doing one's own work in one's own way he had no doubts. His golden laugh, his delight in small things, and the perpetual war of practical jokes that waged between us, was refreshment after working hours. And when we cousins, Phil, his son, Stanley Baldwin and I, went to the beach and came back with descriptions of fat bathers, he would draw them, indescribably swag-bellied, wallowing in the surf. Those were exceedingly good days, and one's work came easily and fully.

Now even in the Bliss Cottage I had a vague notion of an Irish boy, born in India and mixed up with native life. I went as far as to make him the son of a private in an Irish Battalion, and christened him 'Kim of the 'Rishti' — short, that is, for Irish. This done, I felt like Mr. Micawber that I had as good as paid that I. O.U. on the future, and went after other things for some years.

In the meantime my people had left India for good, and were established in a small stone house near Tisbury, Wilts. It possessed a neat little stone-walled stable with a shed or two, all perfectly designed for clay and plaster of Paris works, which are not desired indoors. Later, the Father put up a tin tabernacle which he had thatched, and there disposed his drawing portfolios, big photo and architectural books, gravers, modelling-tools, paints, siccatives, varnishes, and the hundred other don't-you-touch-'ems that every right-minded man who works with his hands naturally collects. (These matters are detailed because they all come into the story.)

Within short walk of him lay Fonthill, the great house of Alfred Morrison, millionaire and collector of all manner of beautiful things, his wife contenting herself with mere precious and sub-precious stones. And my Father was free of all these treasures, and many others in such houses as Clouds, where the Wyndhams lived, a few miles away. I think that both he and my Mother were happy in their English years, for they knew exactly what they did not want; and I knew that when I came over to see them I had no need to sing; 'Backward, turn backward, O Time, in your flight. '

In a gloomy, windy autumn Kim came back to me with insistence, and I took it to be smoked over with my Father. Under our united tobaccos it grew like the Djinn released from the brass bottle, and the more we explored its possibilities the more opulence of detail did we discover. I do not know what proportion of an iceberg is below water-line, but Kim as it finally appeared was about one-tenth of what the first lavish specification called for.

As to its form there was but one possible to the author, who said that what was good enough for Cervantes was good enough for him. To whom the Mother; 'Don't you stand in your wool-boots hiding behind Cervantes with me! You know you couldn't make a plot to save your soul. '

So I went home much fortified and Kim took care of himself. The only trouble was to keep him within bounds. Between us, we knew every step, sight, and smell on his casual road, as well as all the persons he met. Once only, as I remember, did I have to bother the India Office, where there are four acres of books and documents in the basements, for a certain work on Indian magic which I always sincerely regret that I could not steal. They fuss about receipts there.

At 'The Elms, ' Rottingdean, the sou'-wester raged day and night, till the silly windows jiggled their wedges loose. (Which was why the Committee vowed never to have a house of their own with up-and-down windows. Cf. Charles Reade on that subject.) But I was quite unconcerned. I had my Eastern sunlight and if I wanted more I could get it at 'The Gables, ' Tisbury. At last I reported Kim finished. 'Did it stop, or you? 'the Father asked. And when I told him that it was It, he said; 'Then it oughtn't to be too bad. '

He would take no sort of credit for any of his suggestions, memories or confirmations—not even for that single touch of the low-driving sunlight which makes luminous every detail in the picture of the Grand Trunk Road at eventide. The Himalayas I painted all by myself, as the children say. So also the picture of the Lahore Museum of which I had once been Deputy Curator for six weeks—unpaid but immensely important. And there was a half-chapter of the Lama sitting down in the blue-green shadows at the foot of a glacier, telling Kim stories out of the Jatakas, which was truly beautiful but, as my old Classics master would have said, 'otiose, ' and it was removed almost with tears.

But the crown of the fun came when (in 1902) was issued an illustrated edition of my works, and the Father attended to Kim. He had the notion of making low-relief plaques and photographing them afterwards. Here it was needful to catch the local photographer, who, till then, had specialised in privates of the Line with plastered hair and skin-tight uniforms, and to lead him up the strenuous path of photographing dead things so that they might show a little life. The man was a bit bewildered at first, but he had a teacher of teachers, and so grew to understand. The incidental muck-heaps in the stable-yard were quite noticeable, though a loyal housemaid fought them broom-and-bucket, and Mother allowed messy half-born 'sketches' to be dumped by our careless hands on sofas and chairs. Naturally when he got his final proofs he was sure that 'it all ought to be done again from the beginning, ' which was rather how I felt about the letterpress, but, if it be possible, he and I will do that in a better world, and on a scale to amaze Archangels.

There is one picture that I remember of him in the tin tabernacle, hunting big photos of Indian architecture for some utterly trivial detail in a corner of some plaque. He looked up as I came in and, rubbing his beard and carrying on his own thought, quoted; 'If you get simple beauty and naught else, You get about the best thing God invents. ' It is the greatest of my many blessings that I was given grace to know them at the time, instead of having them brought to my remorseful notice too late.

I expect that is why I am perhaps a little impatient over the Higher Cannibalism as practised to-day.

And so much for Kim which has stood up for thirty-five years. There was a good deal of beauty in it, and not a little wisdom; the best in both sorts being owed to my Father.

A great, but frightening, honour came to me when I was thirty-three (1897) and was elected to the Athenaeum under Rule Two, which provides for admitting distinguished persons without ballot. I took counsel with Burne-Jones as to what to do. 'I don't dine there often, ' said he. 'It frightens me rather, but we'll tackle it together. ' And on a night appointed we went to that meal. So far as I recall we were the only people in that big dining-room, for in those days the Athenaeum, till one got to know it, was rather like a cathedral between services. But at any rate I had dined there, and hung my hat on Peg 33. (I have shifted it since.) Before long I realised that if one wanted to know anything from forging an anchor to forging antiquities one would find the world's ultimate expert in the matter at lunch. I managed to be taken into a delightful window-table, pre-empted by an old General, who had begun life as a Middy in the Crimea before he entered the Guards. In his later years he was a fearless yachtsman, as well as several other things, and he dealt faithfully with me when I made technical errors in any tale of mine that interested him. I grew very fond of him, and of four or five others who used that table.

One afternoon, I remember, Parsons of the Turbinia asked if I would care to see a diamond burned. The demonstration took place in a room crammed with wires and electric cells (I forget what their aggregate voltage was) and all went well for a while. The diamond's tip bubbled like cauliflower au gratin. Then there was a flash and a crash, and we were on the floor in darkness. But, as Parsons said, that was not the diamond's fault.

Among other pillars of the dear, dingy, old downstairs billiard-room was Hercules Read, of the British Museum on the Eastern Antiquities side. Externally, he was very handsome, but his professional soul was black, even for that of a Curator—and my Father had been a

Curator. (Note. It is entirely right that the English should mistrust and disregard all the Arts and most of the Sciences, for on that indifference rests their moral grandeur, but their starvation in their estimates is sometimes too marked.)

At this present age I do not lunch very often at the Athenaeum, where it has struck me that the bulk of the members are scandalously young, whether elected under Rule Two or by ballot of their fellow-infants. Nor do I relish persons of forty calling me 'Sir. '

My life made me grossly dependent on Clubs for my spiritual comfort. Three English ones, the Athenaeum, Carlton, and Beefsteak, met my wants, but the Beefsteak gave me most. Our company there was unpredictable, and one could say what one pleased at the moment without being taken at the foot of the letter. Sometimes one would draw a full house of five different professions, from the Bench to the Dramatic Buccaneer. Otherwhiles, three of a kind, chance-stranded in town, would drift into long, leisurely talk that ranged half earth over, and separate well pleased with themselves and their table-companions. And once, when I feared that I might have to dine alone, there entered a member whom I had never seen before, and have never met since, full of bird-preservation. By the time we parted what I did not know about bird sanctuaries was scarcely worth knowing. But it was best when of a sudden some one or something plunged us all in what you might call a general 'rag, ' each man's tongue guarding his own head.

There is no race so dowered as the English with the gift of talking real, rich, allusive, cut-in-and-out 'skittles. ' Americans are too much anecdotards; the French too much orators for this light-handed game, and neither race delivers itself so unreservedly to mirth as we do.

When I lived in Villiers Street, I picked up with the shore-end of a select fishing-club, which met in a tobacconist's back-parlour. They were mostly small tradesmen, keen on roach, dace and such, but they too had that gift, as I expect their forebears had in Addison's time.

The late Doctor Johnson once observed that 'we shall receive no letters in the grave. ' I am perfectly sure, though Boswell never set it down, that he lamented the lack of Clubs in that same place.

Chapter VI

South Africa

But at the back of my head there was an uneasiness, based on things that men were telling me about affairs outside England. (The inhabitants of that country never looked further than their annual seaside resorts.) There was trouble too in South Africa after the Jameson Raid which promised, men wrote me, further trouble. Altogether, one had a sense of 'a sound of a going in the tops of the mulberry trees'—of things moving into position as troops move. And into the middle of it all came the Great Queen's Diamond jubilee, and a certain optimism that scared me. The outcome, as far as I was concerned, took the shape of a set of verses called 'Recessional, ' which were published in The Times in '97 at the end of the Jubilee celebrations. It was more in the nature of a nuzzur-wattu (an averter of the Evil Eye), and—with the conservatism of the English—was used in choirs and places where they sing long after our Navy and Army alike had in the name of 'peace' been rendered innocuous. It was written just before I went off on Navy manoeuvres with my friend Captain E. H. Bayly. When I returned it seemed to me that the time was ripe for its publication, so, after making one or two changes in it, I gave it to The Times. I say 'gave' because for this kind of work I did not take payment. It does not much matter what people think of a man after his death, but I should not like the people whose good opinion I valued to believe that I took money for verses on Joseph Chamberlain, Rhodes, Lord Milner, or any of my South African verse in The Times.

It was this uneasiness of mine which led us down to the Cape in the winter of '97, taking the Father with us. There we lived in a boardinghouse at Wynberg, kept by an Irishwoman, who faithfully followed the instincts of her race and spread miseries and discomforts round her in return for good monies. But the children throve, and the colour, light, and half-oriental manners of the land bound chains round our hearts for years to come.

It was here that I first met Rhodes to have any talk with. He was as inarticulate as a school-boy of fifteen. Jameson and he, as I perceived later, communicated by telepathy. But Jameson was not with him at that time. Rhodes had a habit of jerking out sudden questions as disconcerting as those of a child—or the Roman Emperor he so much resembled. He said to me apropos of nothing in particular; 'What's your dream? ' I answered that he was part of it, and I think I told him that I had come down to look at things. He showed me some of his newly established fruit farms in the peninsula, wonderful old Dutch houses, stalled in deep peace, and lamented the difficulty of getting sound wood for packing-cases and the shortcomings of native labour. But it was his wish and his will that there should be a fruit growing industry in the Colony, and his chosen lieutenants made it presently come to pass. The Colony then owed no thanks to any Dutch Ministry in that regard. The racial twist of the Dutch (they had taken that title to themselves and called the inhabitants of the Low Countries 'Hollanders') was to exploit everything they could which was being done for them, to put every obstacle in the way of any sort of development, and to take all the cash they could squeeze out of it. In which respect they were no better and no worse than many of their brethren. It was against their creed to try and stamp out cattle plagues, to dip their sheep, or to combat locusts, which in a country overwhelmingly pastoral had its drawbacks. Cape Town, as a big distributing centre, was dominated in many ways by rather nervous shopkeepers, who wished to stand well with their customers up-country, and who served as Mayors and occasional public officials. And the aftermath of the Jameson Raid had scared many people.

During the South African War my position among the rank and file came to be unofficially above that of most Generals. Money was wanted to procure small comforts for the troops at the Front and, to this end, the Daily Mail started what must have been a very early 'stunt. ' It was agreed that I should ask the public for subscriptions. That paper charged itself with the rest. My verses ('The Absent-minded Beggar') had some elements of direct appeal but, as was pointed out, lacked 'poetry. ' Sir Arthur Sullivan wedded the words to a tune guaranteed to pull teeth out of barrel-organs. Anybody could do what they chose with the result, recite, sing, intone or reprint, etc., on condition that they turned in all fees and profits to the main account—'The Absentminded Beggar Fund'—which closed at about a quarter of a million. Some of this was spent in tobacco. Men smoked pipes more than cigarettes at that epoch, and the popular brand was a cake—chewable also—called 'Hignett's True Affection. ' My note-of-hand at the Cape Town depot was good for as much as I cared to take about with me. The rest followed. My telegrams were given priority by sweating R. E. sergeants from all sorts of congested depots. My seat in the train was kept for me by British Bayonets in their shirtsleeves. My small baggage was fought for and servilely carried by Colonial details, who are not normally meek, and I was persona gratissima at certain Wynberg Hospitals where the nurses found I was good for pyjamas. Once I took a bale of them to the wrong nurse (the red capes confused me) and, knowing the matter to be urgent, loudly announced; 'Sister, I've got your pyjamas. ' That one was neither grateful nor very polite.

My attractions led to every sort of delightful or sometimes sorrowful wayside intimacies with all manner of men; and only once did I receive a snub. I was going up to Bloemfontein just after its capture in a carriage taken from the Boers, who had covered its floors with sheep's guts and onions, and its side with caricatures of 'Chamberlain' on a gallows. Otherwise, there was nothing much except woodwork. Behind us was an open truck of British troops whom the Company wag was entertaining by mimicking their officers telling them how to pile horseshoes. As evening fell, I got from him a couple of three-wicked, signal-lamp candles, which gave us at least light to eat by. I naturally wanted to know how he had come by these desirable things. He replied; 'Look 'ere, Guv'nor, I didn't ask you 'ow you come by the baccy you dished out just now. Can't you bloody well leave me alone? '

In this same ghost-train an Indian officer's servant (Muhammedan) was worried on a point of conscience. 'Would this Government issued tin of bully-beef be lawful food for a Muslim? ' I told him that, when Islam wars with unbelievers, the Koran permits reasonable latitude of ceremonial obligations; and he need not hesitate. Next dawn, he was at my bunk-side with Anglo-India's morning cup of tea. (He must have stolen the hot water from the engine, for there was not a drop in the landscape.) When I asked how the miracle had come about, he replied, with the smile of my own Kadir Baksh; 'Millar, Sahib, ' signifying that he had found (or 'made') it.

My Bloemfontein trip was on Lord Roberts' order to report and do what I was told. This was explained at the station by two strangers, who grew into my friends for life, H. A. Gwynne, then Head Correspondent of Reuter's, and Perceval Landon of The Times. 'You've got to help us edit a paper for the troops, ' they said, and forth with inducted me into the newly captured 'office, ' for Bloemfontein had fallen—Boer fashion—rather like an outraged Sunday School a few days before.

The compositors and the plant were also captives of our bow and spear and rather cross about it—especially the ex-editor's wife, a German with a tongue. When one saw a compositor, one told him to compose Lord Roberts' Official Proclamation to the deeply injured enemy. I had the satisfaction of picking up from the floor a detailed account of how Her Majesty's Brigade of Guards had been driven into action by the fire of our artillery; and a proof of a really rude leader about myself.

There was in that lull a large trade in proclamations—and butter at half a crown the pound. We used all the old stereos, advertising long-since exhausted comestibles, coal and groceries (facepowder, I think, was the only surviving commodity in the Bloemfontein shops), and we enlivened their interstices with our own contributions, supplemented by the works of dusty men, who looked in and gave us very fine copy—mostly libellous.

Julian Ralph, the very best of Americans, was a co-editor also. And he had a grown son who went down with a fever unpleasantly like typhoid. We searched for a competent doctor, and halted a German who, so great was the terror of our arms after the 'capture, ' demanded haughtily; 'But who shall pay me for my trouble if I come? ' No one seemed to know, but several men explained who would pay him if he dallied on the way. He took one look at the boy's stomach, and said happily; 'Of course it is typhoid. ' Then came the question how to get the case over to hospital, which was rank with typhoid, the Boers having cut the water supply. The first thing was to fetch down the temperature with an alcohol swabbing. Here we were at a standstill till some genius—I think it was Landon—said; 'I've noticed there's an officer's wife in the place who's wearing a fringe. ' On this hint a man went forth into the wide dusty streets, and presently found her, fringe and all. Heaven knows how she had managed to wangle her way up, but she was a sportswoman of purest water. 'Come to my room, ' said she, and in passing over the priceless bottle, only sighed 'Don't use it all—unless you have to. ' We ran the boy down from 103 to a generous 99 and pushed him into hospital, where it turned out that it was not typhoid after all but only bad veldtfever.

First and last there were, I think, eight thousand cases of typhoid in Bloemfontein. Often to my knowledge both 'ceremonial' Union jacks in a battalion would be 'in use 'at the same time. Extra corpses went to the grave under the Service blanket.

Our own utter carelessness, officialdom and ignorance were responsible for much of the deathrate. I have seen a Horse Battery 'dead to the wide' come in at midnight in raging rain and be assigned, by some idiot saving himself trouble, the site of an evacuated typhoid-hospital. Result—thirty cases after a month. I have seen men drinking raw Modder-river a few yards below where the mules were staling; and the organisation and siting of latrines seemed to be considered 'nigger-work. ' The most important medical office in any battalion ought to be Provost-Marshal of Latrines.

To typhoid was added dysentery, the smell of which is even more depressing than the stench of human carrion. One could wind the dysentery tents a mile off. And remember that, till we planted disease, the vast sun-baked land was antiseptic and sterilised—so much so that a clean abdominal Mauser-wound often entailed no more than a week of abstention from solid food. I found this out on a hospital-train, where I had to head off a mob of angry 'abdominals' from regular rations. That was when we were picking up casualties after a small affair called Paardeberg, and the lists—really about two thousand—were carefully minimised to save the English public from 'shock. ' During this work I happened to fall unreservedly, in darkness, over a man near the train, and filled my palms with gravel. He explained in an even voice that he was 'fractured 'ip, sir. 'Ope you ain't 'urt yourself, sir. ' I never got at this unknown Philip Sidney's name. They were wonderful even in the hour of death— these men and boys—lodge-keepers and ex-butlers of the Reserve and raw town-lads of twenty.

But to return to Bloemfontein. In an interval of our editorial labours, I went out of the town and presently met the 'solitary horseman' of the novels. He was a Conductor—Commissariat Sergeant—who reported that the 'flower of the British Army' had been ambushed and cut up at a place called 'Sanna's Post, ' and passed on obviously discomposed. I had imagined the flower of that Army to be busied behind me reading our paper; but, a short while after, I met an officer who, in the old Indian days, was nicknamed 'the Sardine. ' He was calm, but rather fuzzy as to the outlines of his uniform, which was frayed and ripped by bullets. Yes, there had been trouble where he came from, but he was fuller for the moment of professional admiration.

'What was it like? They got us in a donga. Just like going into a theatre. "Stalls left, dress circle right, " don't you know? We just dropped into the trap, and it was "Infantry this way, please. Guns to the right, if you please. " Beautiful bit of work! How many did they get of us? About twelve hundred, I think, and four—maybe six— guns. Expert job they made of it. That's the result of bill-stickin' expeditions. ' And with more compliments to the foe, he too passed on.

By the time that I returned to Bloemfontein the populace had it that eighty thousand Boers were closing in on the town at once, and the Press Censor (Lord Stanley, now Derby) was besieged with persons anxious to telegraph to Cape Town. To him a non-Aryan pushed a domestic wire 'weather here changeable. ' Stanley, himself a little worried for the fate of some of his friends in that ambuscaded column, rebuked the gentleman.

The Sardine was right about the 'bill-sticking' expeditions. Wandering columns had been sent round the country to show how kind the British desired to be to the misguided Boer. But the Transvaal Boer, not being a town-bird, was unimpressed by the 'fall' of the Free State capital, and ran loose on the veldt with his pony and Mauser.

So there had to be a battle, which was called the Battle of Kari Siding. All the staff of the Bloemfontein Friend attended. I was put in a Cape cart, with native driver, containing most of the drinks, and with me was a well-known war-correspondent. The enormous pale landscape swallowed up seven thousand troops without a sign, along a front of seven miles. On our way we passed a collection of neat, deep and empty trenches well undercut for shelter on the shrapnel side. A young Guards officer, recently promoted to Brevet-Major—and rather sore with the paper that we had printed it Branch—studied them interestedly. They were the first dim lines of the dug-out, but his and our eyes were held. The Hun had designed them secundum artem, but the Boer had preferred the open within reach of his pony. At last we came to a lone farm-house in a vale adorned with no less than five white flags. Beyond the ridge was a sputter of musketry and now and then the whoop of a field-piece. 'Here, ' said my guide and guardian, 'we get out and walk. Our driver will wait for us at the farmhouse. ' But the driver loudly objected. 'No, sar. They shoot. They shoot me. ' 'But they are white-flagged all over, ' we said. 'Yess, sar. That why, ' was his answer, and he preferred to take his mules down into a decently remote donga and wait our return.

The farm-house (you will see in a little why I am so detailed) held two men and, I think, two women, who received us disinterestedly. We went on into a vacant world full of sunshine and distances, where now and again a single bullet sang to himself. What I most objected to was the sensation of being under aimed fire—being, as it were, required as a head. 'What are they doing this for? ' I asked my friend. 'Because they think we are the Something Light Horse. They ought to be just under this slope. ' I prayed that the particularly Something Light Horse would go elsewhere, which they presently did, for the aimed fire slackened and a wandering Colonial, bored to extinction, turned up with news from a far flank. 'No; nothing doing and no one to see. ' Then more cracklings and a most cautious move forward to the lip of a large hollow where sheep were grazing. Some of them began to drop and kick. 'That's both sides trying sighting-shots, ' said my companion. 'What range do you make it? ' I asked. 'Eight hundred, at the nearest. That's close quarters nowadays. You'll never see anything closer than this. Modern rifles make it impossible. We're hung up till something cracks somewhere. ' There was a decent lull for meals on both sides, interrupted now and again by sputters. Then one indubitable shell—ridiculously like a pip-squeak in that vastness but throwing up much dirt. 'Krupp! Four or six pounder at extreme range, ' said the expert. 'They still think we're the — Light Horse. They'll come to be fairly regular from now on. ' Sure enough, every twenty minutes or so, one judgmatic shell pitched on our slope. We waited, seeing nothing in the emptiness, and hearing only a faint murmur as of wind along gas-jets, running in and out of the unconcerned hills.

Then pom-poms opened. These were nasty little one-pounders, ten in a belt (which usually jammed about the sixth round). On soft ground they merely thudded. On rock-face the shell breaks up and yowls like a cat. My friend for the first time seemed interested. 'If these are their pom-poms, it's Pretoria for us, ' was his diagnosis. I looked behind me—the whole length of South Africa down to Cape Town—and it seemed very far. I felt that I could have covered it in five minutes under fair conditions, but—not with those aimed shots up my back. The pom-poms opened again at a bare rock-reef that gave the shells full value. For about two minutes a file of racing ponies, their tails and their riders' heads well down, showed and vanished northward. 'Our pom-poms, ' said the correspondent. 'Le Gallais, I expect. Now we shan't be long. ' All this time the absurd Krupp was faithfully feeling for us, vice-Light Horse, and, given a few more hours, might perhaps hit one of us. Then to the left, almost under us, a small piece of hanging woodland filled and fumed with our shrapnel much as a man's moustache fills with cigarette-smoke.

96

It was most impressive and lasted for quite twenty minutes. Then silence; then a movement of men and horses from our side up the slope, and the hangar our guns had been hammering spat steady fire at them. More Boer ponies on more skylines; a last flurry of pom-poms on the right and a little frieze of far-off meek-tailed ponies, already out of rifle range.

'Maffeesh, ' said the correspondent, and fell to writing on his knee. 'We've shifted 'em. '

Leaving our infantry to follow men on ponyback towards the Equator, we returned to the farm-house. In the donga where he was waiting someone squibbed off a rifle just after we took our seats, and our driver flogged out over the rocks to the danger of our sacred bottles.

Then Bloemfontein, and Gwynne storming in late with his accounts complete-one hundred and twenty-five casualties, and the general opinion that 'French was a bit of a butcher' and a tale of the General commanding the cavalry who absolutely refused to break up his horses by gallop ing them across raw rock—'not for any dam' Boer. '

Months later, I got a cutting from an American paper, on information from Geneva—even then a pest-house of propaganda—describing how I and some officers—names, date, and place correct—had entered a farm-house where we found two men and three women. We had dragged the women from under the bed where they had taken refuge (I assure you that no Tantie Sannie of that day could bestow herself beneath any known bed) and, giving them a hundred yards' start, had shot them down as they ran.

Even then, the beastliness struck me as more comic than significant. But by that time I ought to have known that it was the Hun's reflection of his own face as he spied at our back-windows. He had thrown in the 'hundred yards' start' touch as a tribute to our national sense of fair play.

From the business point of view the war was ridiculous. We charged ourselves step by step with the care and maintenance of all Boerdom—women and children included. Whence horrible tales of our atrocities in the concentration-camps.

One of the most widely exploited charges was our deliberate cruelty in making prisoners' tents and quarters open to the north. A Miss Hobhouse among others was loud in this matter, but she was to be excused.

We were showing off our newly-built little 'Woolsack' to a great lady on her way upcountry, where a residence was being built for her. At the larder the wife pointed out that it faced south-that quarter being the coldest when one is south of the Equator. The great lady considered the heresy for a moment. Then, with the British sniff which abolishes the absurd, 'Hmm! I shan't allow that to make any difference to me. '

Some Army and Navy Stores Lists were introduced into the prisoners' camps, and the women returned to civil life with a knowledge of corsets, stockings, toilet-cases, and other accessories frowned upon by their clergymen and their husbands. Qua women they were not very lovely, but they made their men fight, and they knew well how to fight on their own lines.

In the give-and-take of our work our troops got to gauge the merits of the commando-leaders they were facing. As I remember the scale, De Wet, with two hundred and fifty men, was to be taken seriously. With twice that number he was likely to fall over his own feet. Smuts (of Cambridge), warring, men assured me, in a black suit, trousers rucked to the knees, and a top-hat, could handle five hundred but, beyond that, got muddled. And so with the others. I had the felicity of meeting Smuts as a British General, at the Ritz during the Great War. Meditating on things seen and suffered, he said that being hunted about the veldt on a pony made a man think quickly, and that perhaps Mr. Balfour (as he was then) would have been better for the same experience.

Each commando had its own reputation in the field, and the grizzlier their beards the greater our respect. There was an elderly contingent from Wakkerstroom which demanded most cautious handling. They shot, as you might say, for the pot. The young men were not so good. And there were foreign contingents who insisted on fighting after the manner of Europe. These the Boers wisely put in the forefront of the battle and kept away from. In one affair the Zarps—the Transvaal Police—fought brilliantly and were nearly all killed. But they were Swedes for the most part, and we were sorry.

Occasionally foreign prisoners were gathered in. Among them I remember a Frenchman who had joined for pure logical hatred of England, but, being a professional, could not resist telling us how we ought to wage the war. He was quite sound but rather cantankerous.

The 'war' became an unpleasing compost of 'political considerations, ' social reform, and housing; maternity-work and variegated absurdities. It is possible, though I doubt it, that first and last we may have killed four thousand Boers. Our own casualties, mainly from preventible disease, must have been six times as many.

The junior officers agreed that the experience ought to be a 'first-class dress-parade for Armageddon, ' but their practical conclusions were misleading. Long-range, aimed rifle-fire would do the work of the future; troops would never get nearer each other than half a mile, and Mounted Infantry would be vital. This was because, having found men on foot cannot overtake men on ponies, we created eighty thousand of as good Mounted Infantry as the world had seen. For these Western Europe had no use. Artillery preparation of wire-works, such as were not at Magersfontein, was rather overlooked in the reformers' schemes, on account of the difficulty of bringing up ammunition by horse-power. The pom-poms, and Lord Dundonald's galloping light gun-carriages, ate up their own weight in shell in three or four minutes.

In the ramshackle hotel at Bloemfontein, where the correspondents lived and the officers dropped in, one heard free and fierce debate as points came up, but—since no one dreamt of the internal-combustion engine that was to stand the world on its thick head, and since our wireless apparatus did not work in those landscapes—we were all beating the air.

Eventually the 'war' petered out on political lines. Brother Boer— and all ranks called him that—would do everything except die. Our men did not see why they should perish chasing stray commandoes, or festering in block-houses, and there followed a sort of demoralising 'handy-pandy' of alternate surrenders complicated by exchange of Army tobacco for Boer brandy which was bad for both sides.

At long last, we were left apologising to a deeply-indignant people, whom we had been nursing and doctoring for a year or two; and who now expected, and received, all manner of free gifts and appliances for the farming they had never practised. We put them in a position to uphold and expand their primitive lust for racial domination, and thanked God we were 'rid of a knave.'

* * * * *

Into these shifts and changes we would descend yearly for five or six months from the peace of England to the deeper peace of 'The Woolsack,' and life under the oak-trees overhanging the patio, where mother-squirrels taught their babies to climb, and in the stillness of hot afternoons the fall of an acorn was almost like a shot. To one side of us was a pine and eucalyptus grove, heavy with mixed scent; in front our garden, where anything one planted out in May became a blossoming bush by December. Behind all tiered the flank of Table Mountain and its copses of silvertrees, flanking scarred ravines. To get to Rhodes' house, 'Groote Schuur,' one used a path through a ravine set with hydrangeas, which in autumn (England's spring) were one solid packed blue river. To this Paradise we moved each year-end from 1900 to 1907—a complete equipage of governess, maids and children, so that the latter came to know and therefore, as children will, to own the Union Castle Line—stewards and all and on any change of governess to instruct the new hand how cabins were set away for a long voyage and 'what went where.'

Incidentally we lost two governesses and one loved cook by marriage, the tepid seas being propitious to such things.

Ship-board life, going and coming, was a mere prolongation of South Africa and its interests. There were Jews a plenty from the Rand; Pioneers; Native Commissioners dealing with Basutos or Zulus; men of the Matabele Wars and the opening of Rhodesia; prospectors; politicians of all stripes, all full of their business Army officers also, and from one of these, when I expected no such jewel, I got a tale called 'Little Foxes'—so true in detail that an awed Superintendent of Police wrote me out of Port Sudan, demanding how I had come to know the very names of the hounds in the very pack to which he had been Whip in his youth. But, as I wrote him back, I had been talking with the Master.

Jameson, too, once came home with us, and disgraced himself at the table which we kept for ourselves. A most English lady with two fair daughters had been put there our first day out, and when she rightly enough objected to the quality of the food, and called it prison fare, Jameson said; 'Speaking as one of the criminal classes, I assure you it is worse. ' At the next meal the table was all our own.

But the outward journey was the great joy because it always included Christmas near the Line, where there was no room for memories; seasonable inscriptions written in soap on the mirrors by skilly stewards; and a glorious fancydress ball. Then, after the Southern Cross had well risen above the bows, the packing away of heavy kit, secure it would not be needed till May, the friendly, well-known Mountain and the rush to the garden to see what had happened in our absence; the flying barefoot visit to our neighbours the Strubens at Strubenheim, where the children were regularly and lovingly spoiled; the large smile of the Malay laundress, and the easy pick-up-again of existence.

Life went well then, and specially for the children, who had all the beasts on the Rhodes estate to play with. Uphill lived the lions, Alice and Jumbo, whose morning voices were the signal for getting up. The zebra paddock, which the emus also used, was immediately behind 'The Woolsack'—a slope of scores of acres. The zebras were always play-fighting like Lions and Unicorns on the Royal Arms; the game being to grab the other's fore-leg below the knee if it could not snatch it away. No fence could hold them when they cared to shift. Jameson and I once saw a family of three returning from an excursion. A heavy sneeze-wood-post fence and wires lay in the path, blind-tight except where the lowest wire spanned a small ditch. Here Papa kneeled, snouted under the wire till it slid along his withers, hove it up, and so crawled through. Mamma and Baby followed in the same fashion. At this, an aged lawn-mower pony who was watching conceived he might also escape, but got no further than backing his fat hind-quarters against one of the posts, and turning round from time to time in wonder that it had not given way. It was, as Jameson said, the complete allegory of the Boer and the Briton.

In another paddock close to the house lived a spitting llama, whose peculiarity the children learned early. But their little visitors did not, and, if they were told to stand close to the fence and make noises, they did—once. You can see the rest.

But our most interesting visitor was a bull-kudu of some eighteen hands. He would jump the seven-foot fence round our little peach orchard, hook a loaded branch in the great rings of his horns, rend it off with a jerk, eat the peaches, leaving the stones, and lift himself over the wires, like a cloud, up the flank of Table Mountain. Once, coming home after dinner, we met him at the foot of the garden, gigantic in the moonlight, and fetched a compass round him, walking delicately, the warm red dust in our shoes; because we knew that a few days before the keepers had given him a dose of small shot in his stern for chasing somebody's cook.

The children's chaperon on their walks was a bulldog—Jumbo—of terrific aspect, to whom all Kaffirs gave full right of way. There was a legend that he had once taken hold of a native and, when at last removed, came away with his mouth full of native. Normally, he lay about the house and apologised abjectly when anyone stepped on him. The children fed him with currant buns and then, remembering that currants were indigestible, would pick them out of his back teeth while he held his dribbling jaws carefully open.

A baby lion was another of our family for one winter. His mother, Alice, desiring to eat him when born, he was raked out with broomsticks from her side and taken to 'Groote Schuur' where, in spite of the unwilling attentions of a she-dog foster-mother (he had of course the claws of a cat) he pined. The wife hinted that, with care, he might recover. 'Very good, ' said Rhodes. 'I'll send him over to "The Woolsack" and you can try. ' He came, with corrugated-iron den and foster-mother complete. The latter the wife dismissed; went out and bought stout motor-gloves, and the largest of babies' bottles, and fed him forthwith. He highly approved of this, and ceased not to pull at the bottle till it was all empty. His tummy was then slapped, as it might have been a water-melon, to be sure that it rang full, and he went to sleep. Thus he lived and throve in his den, which the children were forbidden to enter, lest their caresses should injure him.

When he was about the size of a large rabbit, he cut little pins of teeth, and made coughing noises which he was persuaded were genuine roars. Later, he developed rickets, and I was despatched to an expert at Cape Town to ask for a cure. 'Too much milk, ' said the expert. 'Give him real, not cold-storage, boiled mutton-broth. ' This at first he refused to touch in the saucer, but was induced to lick the wife's dipped finger, whence he removed the skin. His ears were boxed, and he was left alone with the saucer to learn table-manners. He wailed all night, but in the morning lapped like a lion among Christians, and soon got rid of his infirmity. For three months he was at large among us, incessantly talking to himself as he wandered about the house or in the garden where he stalked butterflies. He dozed on the stoep, I noticed, due north and south, looking with slow eyes up the length of Africa—always a little aloof, but obedient to the children, who at that time wore little more than one garment apiece. We returned him in perfect condition on our departure for England, and he was then the size of a bull-terrier but not so high. Rhodes and Jameson were both away. He was put in a cage, fed, like his family, on imperfectly thawed cold-storage meats fouled in the grit of his floor, and soon died of colic. But M'Slibaan, which we made Matabele for 'Sullivan, ' as fitted his Matabele ancestry, was always honoured among the many kind ghosts that inhabited 'The Woolsack. '

Lions, as pets, are hardly safe after six months old; but here is an exception. A man kept a lioness up-country till she was a full year old, and then, with deep regret on both sides, sent her to Rhodes's Zoo. Six months later he came down, and with a girl who did not know what fear was entered her cage, where she received him fawning, rolling, crooning—almost weeping with love and delight. Theoretically, of course, he and the girl ought to have been killed, but they took no hurt at all.

During the war, by some luck our water-supply had not been restricted, and our bath was of the type you step down into and soak in at full length. Hence also Gwynne, filthy after months of the veldt, standing afar off like a leper. ('I say, I want a bath and—there's my kit in the garden. No, I haven't left it on the stoep. It's crawling. ') Many came. As the children put it: 'There's always lots of dirty ones.'

When Rhodes was hatching his scheme of the Scholarships, he would come over and, as it were, think aloud or discuss, mainly with the wife, the expense side of the idea. It was she who suggested that £250 a year was not enough for scholars who would have to carry themselves through the long intervals of an Oxford 'year. ' So he made it three hundred. My use to him was mainly as a purveyor of words; for he was largely inarticulate. After the idea had been presented—and one had to know his code for it—he would say: 'What am I trying to express? Say it, say it. ' So I would say it, and if the phrase suited not, he would work it over, chin a little down, till it satisfied him.

The order of his life at 'Groote Schuur' was something like this. The senior guest allotted their rooms to men who wished to 'see' him. They did not come except for good reason connected with their work, and they stayed till Rhodes 'saw them, which might be two or three days. His heart compelled him to lie down a good deal on a huge couch on the marble-flagged verandah facing up Table Mountain towards the four-acre patch of hydrangeas, which lay out like lapis-lazuli on the lawns. He would say; 'Well, So-and-so. I see you. What is it? ' And the case would be put.

There was a man laying the Cape-to-Cairo telegraph, who had come to a stretch of seventy miles beside a lake, where the ladies of those parts esteemed copper above gold, and took it from the poles for their adornment. What to do? When he had finished his exposition Rhodes, turning heavily on his couch, said; 'You've got some sort of lake there, haven't you? Lay it like a cable. Don't bother me with a little thing like that. ' Palaver done set, and at his leisure the man returned.

One met interesting folk at 'Groote Schuur' meals, which often ended in long talks of the days of building up Rhodesia.

During the Matabele War Rhodes, with some others, under a guide, had wandered on horseback beyond the limits of safety, and had to take refuge in some caves. The situation was eminently unhealthy, and in view of some angry Matabeles hunting them they had to spur out of it. But the guide, just when the party were in the open, was foolish enough to say something to the effect that Rhodes's 'valuable life' was to be considered. Upon which Rhodes pulled up and said; 'Let's get this straight before we go on. You led us into this mess, didn't you? ' 'Yes, sir, yes. But please come on. ' 'No. Wait a minute. Consequently you're running to save your own hide, aren't you? ' 'Yes, sir. We all are. ' 'That's all right. I only wanted to have it settled. Now we'll come on. ' And they did, but it was a close shave. I heard this at his table, even as I heard his delayed reply to a query by a young officer who wished to know what Rhodes thought of him and his career. Rhodes postponed his answer till dinner and then, in his characteristic voice, laid down that the young man would eminently succeed, but only to a certain point, because he was always thinking of his career and not of the job he was doing. Thirty later years proved the truth of his verdict.

Chapter VII

The Very-Own House

How can I turn from any fire
On any man's hearth-stone?
I know the wonder and desire
That went to build my own.
The Fires.

All this busy while the Committee of Ways and Means kept before them the hope of a house of their very own—a real House in which to settle down for keeps—and took trains on rails and horsed carriages of the age to seek it. Our adventures were many and sometimes grim—as when a 'comfortable nursery' proved to be a dark padded cell at the end of a discreet passage! Thus we quested for two or three years, till one summer day a friend cried at our door; 'Mr. Harmsworth has just brought round one of those motor-car things. Come and try it! '

It was a twenty-minute trip. We returned white with dust and dizzy with noise. But the poison worked from that hour. Somehow, an enterprising Brighton agency hired us a victoria-hooded, carriage-sprung, carriage-braked, single-cylinder, belt-driven, fixed-ignition Embryo which, at times, could cover eight miles an hour. Its hire, including 'driver, ' was three and a half guineas a week. The beloved Aunt, who feared nothing created, said 'Me too! ' So we three house-hunted together taking risks of ignorance that made me shudder through after-years. But we went to Arundel and back, which was sixty miles, and returned in the same ten-hour day! We, and a few other desperate pioneers, took the first shock of outraged public opinion. Earls stood up in their belted barouches and cursed us. Gipsies, governess-carts, brewery waggons—all the world except the poor patient horses who would have been quite quiet if left alone joined in the commination service, and the Times leaders on 'motor-cars' were eolithic in outlook.

Then I bought me a steam-car called a 'Locomobile, ' whose nature and attributes I faithfully drew in a tale called 'Steam Tactics. ' She reduced us to the limits of fatigue and hysteria, all up and down Sussex. Next came the earliest Lanchester, whose springing, even at that time, was perfect. But no designer, manufacturer, owner, nor chauffeur knew anything about anything. The heads of the Lanchester firm would, after furious telegrams, visit us as friends (we were all friends in those days) and sit round our hearth speculating Why What did That. Once, the proud designer—she was his newest baby—took me as far as Worthing, where she fainted opposite a vacant building-lot. This we paved completely with every other fitting that she possessed ere we got at her trouble. We then re-assembled her, a two hours' job. After which, she spat boiling water over our laps, but we stuffed a rug into the geyser and so spouted home.

But it was the heart-breaking Locomobile that brought us to the house called 'Bateman's. ' We had seen an advertisement of her, and we reached her down an enlarged rabbit-hole of a lane. At very first sight the Committee of Ways and Means said; 'That's her! The Only She! Make an honest woman of her—quick! ' We entered and felt her Spirit—her Feng Shui—to be good. We went through every room and found no shadow of ancient regrets, stifled miseries, nor any menace, though the 'new' end of her was three hundred years old. To our woe the Owner said; 'I've just let it for twelve months. ' We withdrew, each repeatedly telling the other that no sensible person would be found dead in the stuffy little valley where she stood. We lied thus while we pretended to look at other houses till, a year later, we saw her advertised again, and got her.

When all was signed and sealed, the seller said; 'Now I can ask you something. How are you going to manage about getting to and from the station? It's nearly four miles, and I've used up two pair of horses on the hill here. ' 'I'm thinking of using this sort of contraption, ' I replied from my seat in—Jane Cakebread Lanchester, I think, was her dishonourable name. 'Oh! Those things haven't come to stay! ' he returned. Years afterwards I met him, and he confided that had he known what I had guessed, he would have asked twice the money. In three years from our purchase the railway station had passed out of our lives. In seven, I heard my chauffeur say to an under-powered visiting sardine-tin; 'Hills? There ain't any hills on the London road. '

The House was not of a type to present to servants by lamp or candle-light. Hence electricity, which in 1902 was a serious affair. We chanced, at a week-end visit, to meet Sir William Willcocks, who had designed the Assouan Dam—a trifling affair on the Nile. Not to be over-crowed, we told him of our project for declutching the water-wheel from an ancient mill at the end of our garden, and using its microscopical mill-pond to run a turbine. That was enough! 'Dam? ' said he. 'You don't know anything about dams or turbines. I'll come and look. ' That Monday morn he came with us, explored the brook and the mill-sluit, and foretold truly the exact amount of horse-power that we should get out of our turbine—'Four and a half and no more. ' But he called me Egyptian names for the state of my brook, which, till then, I had deemed picturesque. 'It's all messed up with trees and bushes. Cut 'em down and slope the banks to one in three. ' 'Lend me a couple of Fellahîn Battalions and I'll begin, ' I said.

He said also; 'Don't run your light cable on poles. Bury it. ' So we got a deep-sea cable which had failed under test at twelve hundred volts—our voltage being one hundred and ten—and laid him in a trench from the Mill to the house, a full furlong, where he worked for a quarter of a century. At the end of that time he was a little fatigued, and the turbine had worn as much as one-sixteenth of an inch on her bearings. So we gave them both honourable demission—and never again got anything so faithful.

Of the little one-street village up the hill we only knew that, according to the guide-books, they came of a smuggling, sheep-stealing stock, brought more or less into civilisation within the past three generations. Those of them who worked for us, and who I presume would to-day be called 'Labour, ' struck for higher pay than they had agreed on as soon as we were committed to our first serious works. My foreman and general contractor, himself of their race, and soon to become our good friend, said; 'They think they've got ye. They think there's no harm in tryin' it. ' There was not. I had sense enough to feel that most of them were artists and craftsmen, either in stone or timber, or wood-cutting, or drain-laying or—which is a gift—the aesthetic disposition of dirt; persons of contrivance who could conjure with any sort of material. As our electric-light campaign developed, a London contractor came down to put a fifteen-inch eductionpipe through the innocent-seeming mill-dam. His imported gang came across a solid core of ancient brickwork about as workable as obsidian. They left, after using very strong words. But every other man of 'our folk' had known exactly where and what that core was, and when 'Lunnon' had sufficiently weakened it, they 'conjured' the pipe quietly through what remained.

The only thing that ever shook them was when we cut a little under the Mill foundations to fix the turbine; and found that she sat on a crib or raft of two-foot-square elm logs. What we took came out, to all appearance, as untouched as when it had been put under water. Yet, in an hour, the great baulk, exposed to air, became silver dust, and the men stood round marvelling. There was one among them, close upon seventy when we first met, a poacher by heredity and instinct, a gentleman who, when his need to drink was on him, which was not too often, absented himself and had it out alone; and he was more 'one with Nature' than whole parlours full of poets. He became our special stay and counsellor. Once we wanted to shift a lime and a witch-elm into the garden proper. He said not a word till we talked of getting a tree-specialist from London. 'Have it as you're minded. I dunno as I should if I was you, ' was his comment. By this we understood that he would take charge when the planets were favourable. Presently, he called up four of his own kin (also artists) and brushed us aside. The trees came away kindly. He placed them, with due regard for their growth for the next two or three generations; supported them, throat and bole, with stays and stiffenings, and bade us hold them thus for four years. All fell out as he had foretold. The trees are now close on forty foot high and have never flinched. Equally, a well grown witch-elm that needed discipline, he climbed into and topped, and she carries to this day the graceful dome he gave her. In his later years—he lived to be close on eighty-five—he would, as I am doing now, review his past, which held incident enough for many unpublishable volumes. He spoke of old loves, fights, intrigues, anonymous denunciations 'by such folk as knew writing, ' and vindictive conspiracies carried out with oriental thoroughness. Of poaching he talked in all its branches, from buying Cocculus Indicus for poisoning fish in ponds, to the art of making silk-nets for trout-brooks—mine among them, and he left a specimen to me; and of pitched battles (guns barred) with heavy-handed keepers in the old days in Lord Ashburnham's woods where a man might pick up a fallow deer. His sagas were lighted with pictures of Nature as he, indeed, knew her; night-pieces and dawn-breakings; stealthy returns and the thinking out of alibis, all naked by the fire, while his clothes dried; and of the face and temper of the next twilight under which he stole forth to follow his passion. His wife, after she had known us for ten years, would range through a past that accepted magic, witchcraft and love-philtres, for which last there was a demand as late as the middle 'sixties.

She described one midnight ritual at the local 'wise woman's' cottage, when a black cock was killed with curious rites and words, and 'all de time dere was, like, someone trying to come through at ye from outside in de dark. Dunno as I believe so much in such things now, but when I was a maid I—I justabout did! ' She died well over ninety, and to the last carried the tact, manner and presence, for all she was so small, of an old-world Duchess.

There were interesting and helpful outsiders, too. One was a journeyman bricklayer who, I remember, kept a store of gold sovereigns loose in his pocket, and kindly built us a wall; but so leisurely that he came to be almost part of the establishment. When we wished to sink a well opposite some cottages, he said he had the gift of water-finding, and I testify that, when he held one fork of the hazel Y and I the other, the thing bowed itself against all the grip of my hand over an unfailing supply.

Then, out of the woods that know everything and tell nothing, came two dark and mysterious Primitives. They had heard. They would sink that well, for they had the 'gift. ' Their tools were an enormous wooden trug, a portable windlass whose handles were curved, and smooth as ox-horns, and a short-handled hoe. They made a ring of brickwork on the bare ground and, with their hands at first, grubbed out the dirt beneath it. As the ring sank they heightened it, course by course, grubbing out with the hoe, till the shaft, true as a rifle-barrel, was deep enough to call for their Father of Trugs, which one brother down below would fill, and the other haul up on the magic windlass. When we stopped, at twenty-five feet, we had found a Jacobean tobacco-pipe, a worn Cromwellian latten spoon and, at the bottom of all, the bronze cheek of a Roman horse-bit.

In cleaning out an old pond which might have been an ancient marl-pit or mine-head, we dredged two intact Elizabethan 'sealed quarts' that Christopher Sly affected, all pearly with the patina of centuries. Its deepest mud yielded us a perfectly polished Neolithic axe-head with but one chip on its still venomous edge.

These things are detailed that you may understand how, when my cousin, Ambrose Poynter, said to me; 'Write a yarn about Roman times here, ' I was interested. 'Write, ' said he, 'about an old Centurion of the Occupation telling his experiences to his children. ' 'What is his name? ' I demanded, for I move easiest from a given point. 'Parnesius, ' said my cousin; and the name stuck in my head. I was then on Committee of Ways and Means (which had grown to include Public Works and Communications) but, in due season, the name came back—with seven other inchoate devils. I went off Committee, and began to 'hatch, ' in which state I was 'a brother to dragons and a companion to owls. ' Just beyond the west fringe of our land, in a little valley running from Nowhere to Nothing-at-all, stood the long, overgrown slag-heap of a most ancient forge, supposed to have been worked by the Phoenicians and Romans and, since then, uninterruptedly till the middle of the eighteenth century. The bracken and rush-patches still hid stray pigs of iron, and if one scratched a few inches through the rabbit-shaven turf, one came on the narrow mule-tracks of peacock-hued furnace-slag laid down in Elizabeth's day. The ghost of a road climbed up out of this dead arena, and crossed our fields, where it was known as 'The Gunway, ' and popularly connected with Armada times. Every foot of that little corner was alive with ghosts and shadows. Then, it pleased our children to act for us, in the open, what they remembered of A Midsummer-Night's Dream. Then a friend gave them a real birchbark canoe, drawing at least three inches, in which they went adventuring on the brook. And in a near pasture of the water-meadows lay out an old and unshifting Fairy Ring.

You see how patiently the cards were stacked and dealt into my hands? The Old Things of our Valley glided into every aspect of our outdoor works. Earth, Air, Water and People had been—I saw it at last—in full conspiracy to give me ten times as much as I could compass, even if I wrote a complete history of England, as that might have touched or reached our Valley.

I went off at score—not on Parnesius, but a story told in a fog by a petty Baltic pirate, who had brought his galley to Pevensey and, off Beachy Head—where in the War we heard merchant ships being torpedoed—had passed the Roman fleet abandoning Britain to her doom. That tale may have served as a pipe-opener, but one could not see its wood for its trees, so I threw it away.

I carried the situation to the little house in Wiltshire, where my Father and Mother were installed; and smoked it over with the Father, who said—not for the first time; 'Most things in this world are accomplished by judicious leaving alone. ' So we played cribbage (he had carved a perfect Lama and a little Kim for my two pegs), while the Mother worked beside us, or, each taking a book, lapsed into the silence of entire mutual comprehension. One night, apropos of nothing at all, the Father said; 'And you'll have to look up your references rather more carefully, won't you? ' That had not been my distinction on the little Civil and Military.

This led me on another false scent. I wrote a tale told by Daniel Defoe in a brickyard (we had a real one of our own at that time where we burned bricks for barns and cottages to the exact tints we desired) of how he had been sent to stampede King James II, then havering about Thames mouth, out of an England where no party had any use for him. It turned out a painstaken and meritorious piece of work, overloaded with verified references, with about as much feeling to it as a walking-stick. So it also was discarded, with a tale of Doctor Johnson telling the children how he had once thrown his spurs out of a boat in Scotland, to the amazement of one Boswell. Evidently my Daemon would not function in brickyards or schoolrooms. Therefore, like Alice in Wonderland, I turned my back on the whole thing and walked the other way. Therefore, the whole thing set and linked itself. I fell first upon Normans and Saxons. Parnesius came later, directly out of a little wood above the Phoenician forge; and the rest of the tales in Puck of Pook's Hill followed in order. The Father came over to see us and, hearing 'Hal o' the Draft, ' closed in with fore-reaching pen, presently ousted me from my table, and inlaid the description of Hal's own drawing-knife. He liked that tale, and its companion piece 'The Wrong Thing' (Rewards and Fairies), which latter he embellished, notably in respect to an Italian fresco-worker, whose work never went 'deeper than the plaster. ' He said that 'judicious leaving alone' did not apply between artists.

Of 'Dymchurch Flit, ' with which I was always unashamedly content, he asked; 'Where did you get that lighting from? It had come of itself. Qua workmanship, that tale and two night-pieces in 'Cold Iron' (Rewards and Fairies) are the best in that kind I have ever made, but somehow 'The Treasure and the Law' (Puck of Pook's Hill) always struck me as too heavy for its frame.

Yet that tale brought me a prized petty triumph. I had put a well into the wall of Pevensey Castle circa A. D. 1100, because I needed it there. Archaeologically, it did not exist till this year (1935) when excavators brought such a well to light. But that I maintain was a reasonable gamble. Self-contained castles must have self-contained water supplies. A longer chance that I took in my Roman tales was when I quartered the Seventh Cohort of the Thirtieth (Ulpia Victrix) Legion on the Wall, and asserted that there Roman troops used arrows against the Picts. The first shot was based on honest 'research'; the second was legitimate inference. Years after the tale was told, a digging-party on the Wall sent me some heavy four-sided, Roman-made, 'killing' arrows found in situ and—most marvellously—a rubbing of a memorial-tablet to the Seventh Cohort of the Thirtieth Legion! Having been brought up in a suspicious school, I suspected a 'leg-pull' here, but was assured that the rubbing was perfectly genuine.

I embarked on Rewards and Fairies—the second book—in two minds. Stories a plenty I had to tell, but how many would be authentic and how many due to 'induction'? There was moreover the old Law; 'As soon as you find you can do anything, do something you can't. '

My doubt cleared itself with the first tale, 'Cold Iron, ' which gave me my underwood; 'What else could I have done? '—the plinth of all structures. Yet, since the tales had to be read by children, before people realised that they were 'meant for grown-ups; and since they had to be a sort of balance to, as well as a seal upon, some aspects of my 'Imperialistic' output in the past, I worked the material in three or four overlaid tints and textures, which might or might not reveal themselves according to the shifting light of sex, youth, and experience. It was like working lacquer and mother-o'-pearl, a natural combination, into the same scheme as niello and grisaille, and trying not to let the joins show.

So I loaded the book up with allegories and allusions, and verified references until my old Chief would have been almost pleased with me; put in three or four really good sets of verses; the bones of one entire historical novel for any to clothe who cared; and even slipped in a cryptogram, whose key I regret I must have utterly forgotten. It was glorious fun; and I knew it must be very good or very bad because the series turned itself off just as Kim had done.

Among the verses in Rewards was one set called 'If— —', which escaped from the book, and for a while ran about the world. They were drawn from Jameson's character, and contained counsels of perfection most easy to give. Once started, the mechanisation of the age made them snowball themselves in a way that startled me. Schools, and places where they teach, took them for the suffering

114

Young—which did me no good with the Young when I met them later. ('Why did you write that stuff? I've had to write it out twice as an impot. ') They were printed as cards to hang up in offices and bedrooms; illuminated text-wise and anthologised to weariness. Twenty-seven of the Nations of the Earth translated them into their seven-and-twenty tongues, and printed them on every sort of fabric.

Some years after the War a kind friend hinted that my two innocent little books might have helped towards begetting the 'Higher Cannibalism' in biography. By which I understood him to mean the exhumation of scarcely cold notorieties, defenceless females for choice, and tricking them out with sprightly inferences and 'sex'- deductions to suit the mood of the market. It was an awful charge, and anyway I felt that others had qualified as Chief Morticians to that trade.

For rest and refreshment and dearly-loved experiments and anxieties, during the six months or so of each year that we stayed in England, there was always the House and the land, and on occasion the Brook at the foot of our garden, which would flood devastatingly. As she supplied the water for our turbine, and as the little weir which turned her current into the little mill-race was of a frail antiquity, one had to attend to her often and at once, and always at the most inconvenient moment.

Undiscerning folks would ask; 'What do you find to do in the country? ' 'Our answer was 'Everything except time to do it. '

We began with tenants—two or three small farmers on our very few acres—from whom we learned that farming was a mixture of farce, fraud, and philanthropy that stole the heart out of the land. After many, and some comic experiences, we fell back on our own county's cattle—the big, red Sussex breed who make beef and not milk. One got something at least for one's money from the mere sight of them, and they did not tell lies. Rider Haggard would visit us from time to time and give of his ample land-wisdom. I remember I planted some new apple-trees in an old orchard then rented by an Irishman, who at once put in an agile and hungry goat. Haggard met

115

the combination suddenly one morning. He had gifts of speech, and said very clearly indeed that one might as well put Satan in an orchard as a goat. I forget what—though I acted on it—he said about tenants. His comings were always a joy to us and the children, who followed him like hounds in the hope of 'more South African stories. ' Never was a better tale-teller or, to my mind, a man with a more convincing imagination. We found by accident that each could work at ease in the other's company. So he would visit me, and I him, with work in hand; and between us we could even hatch out tales together—a most exacting test of sympathy.

I was honoured till he died by the friendship of a Colonel Wemyss Feilden, who moved into the village to inherit a beautiful little William and Mary house on the same day as we came to take over 'Bateman's. ' He was in soul and spirit Colonel Newcome; in manner as diffident and retiring as an old maid out of Cranford; and up to his eighty-second year could fairly walk me off my feet, and pull down pheasants from high heaven. He had begun life in the Black Watch, with whom, outside Delhi during the Mutiny, he heard one morning as they were all shaving that a 'little fellow called Roberts' had captured single-handed a rebel Standard and was coming through the Camp. 'We all turned out. The boy was on horseback looking rather pleased with himself, and his mounted Orderly carried the Colour behind him. We cheered him with the lather on our faces. '

After the Mutiny he sold out, and having interests in Natal went awhile to South Africa. Next, he ran the blockade of the U. S. Civil War, and wedded his Southern wife in Richmond with a ring hammered out of an English sovereign 'because there wasn't any gold in Richmond just then. ' Mrs. Feilden at seventy-five was in herself fair explanation of all the steps he had taken—and forfeited.

He came to be one of Lee's aides-de-camp, and told me how once on a stormy night, when he rode in with despatches, Lee had ordered him to take off his dripping cloak and lie by the fire; and how when he waked from badly needed sleep, he saw the General on his knees before the flame drying the cloak. 'That was just before the

116

surrender, ' said he. 'We had finished robbing the grave, and we'd begun on the cradle. For those last three months I was with fifteen thousand boys under seventeen, and I don't remember any one of them even smiling. '

Bit by bit I came to understand that he was a traveller and an Arctic explorer, in possession of the snow-white Polar ribbon; a botanist and naturalist of reputation; and himself above all.

When Rider Haggard heard these things, he rested not till he had made the Colonel's acquaintance. They cottoned to each other on sight and sound; South Africa in the early days being their bond. One evening, Haggard told us how his son had been born on the edge of Zulu, I think, territory, the first white child in those parts. 'Yes, ' said the Colonel, quietly out of his corner. 'I and'—he named two men—'rode twenty-seven miles to look at him. We hadn't seen a white baby for some time. ' Then Haggard remembered that visit of strangers.

And once there came to us with her married daughter the widow of a Confederate Cavalry leader; both of them were what you might call 'unreconstructed' rebels. Somehow, the widow mentioned a road and a church beside a river in Georgia. 'It's still there, then? ' said the Colonel, giving it its name. 'Why do you ask? 'was the quick reply. ' Because, if you look in such-and-such a pew, you might find my initials. I cut them there the night — —'s Cavalry stabled their horses there. ' There was a pause. ''Fore God, then, who are you? ' she gasped. He told her. 'You knew my husband? ' 'I served under him. He was the only man in our corps who wore a white collar. ' She pelted him with questions, and the names of the old dead. 'Come away, ' whispered her daughter to me. 'They don't want us. ' Nor did they for a long hour.

Sooner or later, all sorts of men cast up at our house. From India naturally; from the Cape increasingly after the Boer War and our half-yearly visits there; from Rhodesia when that province was in the making; from Australia, with schemes for emigration which one knew Organised Labour would never allow to pass its legislatures;

from Canada, when 'Imperial Preference' came to the fore, and Jameson, after one bitter experience, cursed 'that dam' dancingmaster (Laurier) who had bitched the whole show'; and from off main-line Islands and Colonies—men of all makes, each with his lifetale, grievance, idea, ideal, or warning.

There was an ex-Governor of the Philippines, who had slaved his soul out for years to pull his charge into some sort of shape and—on a turn of the political wheel at Washington—had been dismissed at literally less notice than he would have dared to give a native orderly. I remembered not a few men whose work and hope had been snatched from under their noses, and my sympathy was very real. His account of Filipino political 'leaders, ' writing and shouting all day for 'independence' and running round to him after dark to be assured that there was no chance of the dread boon being granted— 'because then we shall most probably all be killed'—was cheeringly familiar.

The difficulty was to keep these interests separate in the head; but the grind of adjusting the mental eye to new perspectives was good for the faculties. Besides this viva voce, there was always heavy written work, three-fourths of which was valueless, but for the sake of the possibly worth-while residue all had to be gone through. This was specially the case during the three years before the War, when warnings came thick and fast, and the wise people to whom I conveyed them said; 'Oh, but you're so-o—extreme. '

Blasts of extravagant publicity alternated with my office-work. In the late summer of '06, for example, we took ship to Canada, which I had not seen in any particularity for many years, and of which I had been told that it was coming out of its spiritual and material subjection to the United States. Our steamer was an Allan Liner with the earliest turbines and wireless. In the wirelessroom, as we were feeling our way blind through the straits of Belle Isle, a sister ship, sixty miles ahead, morsed that the fog with her was even thicker. Said a young engineer in the doorway 'Who's yon talking, Jock? Ask him if he's done drying his socks. ' And the old professional jest crackled out through the smother. It was my first experience of practical wireless.

At Quebec we met Sir William Van Horne, head of the whole C. P.R. system, but, on our wedding trip fifteen years before, a mere Divisional Superintendent who had lost a trunk of my wife's and had stood his Division on its head to find it. His deferred, but ample revenge was to give us one whole Pullman car with coloured porter complete, to take and use and hitch on to and declutch from any train we chose, to anywhere we fancied, for as long as we liked. We took it, and did all those things to Vancouver and back again. When we wished to sleep in peace, it slid off into still, secret freight-yards till morning. When we would eat, chefs of the great mail trains, which it had honoured by its attachment, asked us what we would like. (It was the season of blueberries and wild duck.) If we even looked as though we wanted anything, that thing would be waiting for us a few score miles up the line. In this manner and in such state we progressed, and the procession and the progress was meat and drink to the soul of William the coloured porter, our Nurse, Valet, Seneschal, and Master of Ceremonies. (More by token, the wife understood coloured folk, and that put William all at ease.) Many people would come aboard to visit us at halting-places, and there were speeches of sorts to be prepared and delivered at the towns. In the first case; "Nother depytation, Boss, ' from William behind enormous flower-pieces; 'and more bo-kays for de Lady. ' In the second; 'Dere's a speech doo at — —. You go right ahaid with what you're composin', Boss. Jest put your feets out an' I'll shine 'em meanwhile. ' So, brushed up and properly shod, I was ushered into the public eye by the immortal William.

In some ways it was punishing 'all out' work, but in all ways worth it. I had been given an honorary Degree, my first, by the McGill University at Montreal. That University received me with interest, and after I had delivered a highly moral discourse, the students dumped me into a fragile horse-vehicle, which they hurtled through the streets. Said one nice child sitting in the hood of it; 'You gave us a dam' dull speech. Can't you say anything amusin' now? ' I could but express my fears for the safety of the conveyance, which was disintegrating by instalments.

In '15 I met some of those boys digging trenches in France.

No words of mine can give any notion of the kindness and good-will lavished on us through every step of our road. I tried, and failed to do so in a written account of it. (Letters to the Family.) And always the marvel—to which the Canadians seemed insensible—was that on one side of an imaginary line should be Safety, Law, Honour, and Obedience, and on the other frank, brutal decivilisation; and that, despite this, Canada should be impressed by any aspect whatever of the United States. Some hint of this too I strove to give in my Letters.

Before we parted, William told us a tale of a friend of his who was consumed with desire to be a Pullman porter 'bekase he had watched me doin' it, an' thought he could do it—jest by watchin' me. ' (This was the burden of his parable, like a deep-toned locomotive bell.) Overborne at last, William wangled for his friend the coveted post—'next car ahaid to mine . .. I got my folks to baid early 'kase I guessed he'd be needin' me soon. . .. But he thought he could do it. And den all his folk in his car, dey all wanted to go to baid at de same time—like dey allus do. An' he tried—Gawd knows he tried— to 'commodate 'em all de same time an' he couldn't. He jes' couldn't. . .. He didn't know haow. He thought he did bekase he had, ' etc. etc. 'An' den he quit . .. he jes' quit. ' Along pause.

'Jumped out of window? ' we demanded.

'No. Oh no. Dey wasn't no jump to him dat night. He went into de broom-closet—'kase I found him dar—an' he cried, an' all his folks slammin' on de broom-house door an' cussin' him 'kase dey wanted to go to baid. An' he couldn't put 'em dar. He couldn't put 'em. He thought, ' etc. etc. 'An' den? Why, o' course I jes' whirled in an' put 'em to baid for him an' when I told 'em how t'wuz with dat sorerful cryin' nigger, dey laughed. Dey laughed heaps an' heaps. . .. But he thought he could do it by havin' watched me do it. '

A few weeks after we returned from the wonderful trip, I was notified that I had been awarded the Nobel Prize of that year for Literature. It was a very great honour, in all ways unexpected.

It was necessary to go to Stockholm. Even while we were on the sea, the old King of Sweden died. We reached the city, snow-white under sun, to find all world in evening dress, the official mourning, which is curiously impressive. Next afternoon, the prize-winners were taken to be presented to the new King. Winter darkness in those latitudes falls at three o'clock, and it was snowing. One half of the vast acreage of the Palace sat in darkness, for there lay the dead King's body. We were conveyed along interminable corridors looking out into black quadrangles, where snow whitened the cloaks of the sentries, the breeches of old-time cannon, and the shotpiles alongside of them. Presently, we reached a living world of more corridors and suites all lighted up, but wrapped in that Court hush which is like no other silence on earth. Then, in a great lit room, the weary-eyed, overworked, new King, saying to each the words appropriate to the occasion. Next, the Queen, in marvellous Mary Queen of Scots mourning, a few words, and the return piloted by soft-footed Court officials through a stillness so deep that one heard the click of the decorations on their uniforms. They said that the last words of the old King had been 'Don't let them shut the theatres for me. ' So Stockholm that night went soberly about her pleasures, all dumbed down under the snow.

Morning did not come till ten o'clock; and one lay abed in thick dark, listening to the blunted grind of the trams speeding the people to their work-day's work. But the ordering of their lives was reasonable, thought out, and most comfortable for all classes in the matters of food, housing, the lesser but more desirable decencies, and the consideration given to the Arts. I had only known the Swede as a first-class immigrant in various parts of the earth. Looking at his native land I could guess whence he drew his strength and directness. Snow and frost are no bad nurses.

At that epoch staid women attached to the public wash-houses washed in a glorious lather of soap, worked up with big bunches of finest pine-shavings (when you think of it, a sponge is almost as dirty a tool as the permanent tooth-brush of the European), men desirous of the most luxurious bath known to civilisation. But foreigners did not always catch the idea. Hence this tale told to me at a winter resort in the deep, creamy contralto of the North by a Swedish lady who took, and pronounced, her English rather biblically. The introit you can imagine for yourself. Here is the finale; 'And then she—the old woman com-ed—came—in to wash that man. But he was angered—angry. He wented—he went dee-ep into the water and he say-ed—said—"Go a-way! " And she sayed, "But I comm to wash you, sare. " And she made to do that. But he tur-ned over up-on his fa-ace, and wa-ved his legs in the airs and he sayed, "Go a-dam-way away! " So she went to the Direktor and she say-ed "Comm he-ere. There are a mads in my bath, which will not let me wash of him. " But the Direktor say-ed to her; "Oh, that are not a mads. That are an Englishman. He will himself—he will wash himself. "'

Chapter VIII

Working-Tools

Every man must be his own law in his own work, but it is a poor-spirited artist in any craft who does not know how the other man's work should be done or could be improved. I have heard as much criticism among hedgers and ditchers and woodmen of a companion's handling of spade, bill-hook, or axe, as would fill a Sunday paper. Carters and cattle-men are even more meticulous, since they must deal with temperaments and seasonal instabilities. We had once on the farms a pair of brothers between ten and twelve. The younger could deal so cunningly with an intractable cart-mare who rushed her gates, and for choice diagonally, that he was called in to take charge of her as a matter of course. The elder, at eleven, could do all that his strength allowed, and the much more that ancestral craft had added, with any edged tool or wood. Modern progress has turned them into meritorious menials.

One of my cattle-men had a son who at eight could appraise the merits and character of any beast in his father's care, and was on terms of terrifying familiarity with the herd-bull, whom he would slap on the nose to make him walk disposedly before us when visitors came. At eighteen, he would have been worth two hundred a year to begin with on any ranch in the Dominions. But he was 'good at his books, ' and is now in a small grocery, but wears a black coat on the Sabbath. Which things are a portent.

I have told what my early surroundings were, and how richly they furnished me with material. Also, how rigorously newspaper spaces limited my canvases and, for the reader's sake, prescribed that within these limits must be some sort of beginning, middle, and end. My ordinary reporting, leader- and note-writing carried the same lesson, which took me an impatient while to learn. Added to this, I was almost nightly responsible for my output to visible and often brutally voluble critics at the Club. They were not concerned with my dreams. They wanted accuracy and interest, but first of all accuracy.

My young head was in a ferment of new things seen and realised at every turn and—that I might in any way keep abreast of the flood— it was necessary that every word should tell, carry, weigh, taste and, if need were, smell. Here the Father helped me incomparably by his 'judicious leaving alone. ' 'Make your own experiments, ' said he. 'It's the only road. If I helped, I'd hinder. ' So I made my own experiments and, of course, the viler they were the more I admired them.

Mercifully, the mere act of writing was, and always has been, a physical pleasure to me. This made it easier to throw away anything that did not turn out well: and to practise, as it were, scales.

Verse, naturally, came first, and here the Mother was at hand, with now and then some shrivelling comment that infuriated me. But, as she said; 'There's no Mother in Poetry, my dear. ' It was she, indeed, who had collected and privately printed verses written at school up to my sixteenth year, which I faithfully sent out from the little House of the Dear Ladies. Later, when the notoriety came, 'in they broke, those people of importance, ' and the innocent thing 'came on to the market, ' and Philadelphia lawyers, a breed by itself, wanted to know, because they had paid much money for an old copy, what I remembered about its genesis. They had been first written in a stiff, marble-backed MS. book, the front page of which the Father had inset with a scandalous sepia-sketch of Tennyson and Browning in procession, and a spectacled schoolboy bringing up the rear. I gave it, when I left school, to a woman who returned it to me many years later—for which she will take an even higher place in Heaven than her natural goodness ensures—and I burnt it, lest it should fall into the hands of 'lesser breeds without the (Copyright) law. '

I forget who started the notion of my writing a series of Anglo-Indian tales, but I remember our council over the naming of the series. They were originally much longer than when they appeared, but the shortening of them, first to my own fancy after rapturous re-

readings, and next to the space available, taught me that a tale from which pieces have been raked out is like a fire that has been poked. One does not know that the operation has been performed, but every one feels the effect. Note, though, that the excised stuff must have been honestly written for inclusion. I found that when, to save trouble, I 'wrote short' ab initio much salt went out of the work. This supports the theory of the chimaera which, having bombinated and been removed, is capable of producing secondary causes in vacuo.

This leads me to the Higher Editing. Take of well-ground Indian Ink as much as suffices and a camel-hair brush proportionate to the inter-spaces of your lines. In an auspicious hour, read your final draft and consider faithfully every paragraph, sentence and word, blacking out where requisite. Let it lie by to drain as long as possible. At the end of that time, re-read and you should find that it will bear a second shortening. Finally, read it aloud alone and at leisure. Maybe a shade more brushwork will then indicate or impose itself. If not, praise Allah and let it go, and 'when thou hast done, repent not. ' The shorter the tale, the longer the brushwork and, normally, the shorter the lie-by, and vice versa. The longer the tale, the less brush but the longer lie-by. I have had tales by me for three or five years which shortened themselves almost yearly. The magic lies in the Brush and the Ink. For the Pen, when it is writing, can only scratch; and bottled ink is not to compare with the ground Chinese stick. Experto crede.

Let us now consider the Personal Daemon of Aristotle and others, of whom it has been truthfully written, though not published: —

This is the doom of the Makers—their Daemon lives in their pen. If he be absent or sleeping, they are even as other men. But if he be utterly present, and they swerve not from his behest, The word that he gives shall continue, whether in earnest or jest.

Most men, and some most unlikely, keep him under an alias which varies with their literary or scientific attainments. Mine came to me early when I sat bewildered among other notions, and said; 'Take this and no other. ' I obeyed, and was rewarded. It was a tale in the little Christmas magazine Quartette which we four wrote together, and it was called 'The Phantom 'Rickshaw. ' Some of it was weak, much was bad and out of key; but it was my first serious attempt to think in another man's skin.

After that I learned to lean upon him and recognise the sign of his approach. If ever I held back, Ananias fashion, anything of myself (even though I had to throw it out afterwards) I paid for it by missing what I then knew the tale lacked. As an instance, many years later I wrote about a mediaeval artist, a monastery, and the premature discovery of the microscope. ('The Eye of Allah. ') Again and again it went dead under my hand, and for the life of me I could not see why. I put it away and waited. Then said my Daemon—and I was meditating something else at the time—'Treat it as an illuminated manuscript. ' I had ridden off on hard black-and-white decoration, instead of pumicing the whole thing ivory-smooth, and loading it with thick colour and gilt. Again, in a South African, post-Boer War tale called 'The Captive, ' which was built up round the phrase 'a first-class dress-parade for Armageddon, ' I could not get my lighting into key with the tone of the monologue. The background insisted too much. My Daemon said at last 'Paint the background first once for all, as hard as a public-house sign, and leave it alone. ' This done, the rest fell into place with the American accent and outlook of the teller.

My Daemon was with me in the Jungle Books, Kim, and both Puck books, and good care I took to walk delicately, lest he should withdraw. I know that he did not, because when those books were finished they said so themselves with, almost, the water-hammer click of a tap turned off. One of the clauses in our contract was that I should never follow up 'a success, ' for by this sin fell Napoleon and a few others. Note here. When your Daemon is in charge, do not try to think consciously. Drift, wait, and obey.

I am afraid that I was not much impressed by reviews. But my early days in London were unfortunate. As I got to know literary circles and their critical output, I was struck by the slenderness of some of the writers' equipment. I could not see how they got along with so casual a knowledge of French work and, apparently, of much English grounding that I had supposed indispensable. Their stuff seemed to be a day-to-day traffic in generalities, hedged by trade considerations. Here I expect I was wrong, but, making my own tests (the man who had asked me out to dinner to discover what I had read gave me the notion), I would ask simple questions, misquote or misattribute my quotations; or (once or twice) invent an author. The result did not increase my reverence. Had they been newspaper men in a hurry, I should have understood; but the gentlemen were presented to me as Priests and Pontiffs. And the generality of them seemed to have followed other trades—in banks or offices—before coming to the Ink; whereas I was free born. It was pure snobism on my part, but it served to keep me inside myself, which is what snobbery is for.

I would not to-day recommend any writer to concern himself overly with reviews. London is a parish, and the Provincial Press has been syndicated, standardised, and smarmed down out of individuality. But there remains still a little fun in that fair. In Manchester was a paper called The Manchester Guardian. Outside the mule-lines I had never met anything that could kick or squeal so continuously, or so completely round the entire compass of things. It suspected me from the first, and when my 'Imperialistic' iniquities were established after the Boer War, it used each new book of mine for a shrill recount of my previous sins (exactly as C—— used to do) and, I think, enjoyed itself. In return I collected and filed its more acid but uncommonly well-written leaders for my own purposes. After many years, I wrote a tale ('The Wish House') about a woman of what was called 'temperament' who loved a man and who also suffered from a cancer on her leg—the exact situation carefully specified. The review came to me with a gibe on the margin from a faithful friend; 'You threw up a catch that time! ' The review said that I had revived Chaucer's Wife of Bath even to the 'mormal on her shinne. ' And it looked just like that too! There was no possible answer, so, breaking my rule not to have commerce with any paper, I wrote to the Manchester Guardian and gave myself 'out—-caught to leg. ' The reply came from an evident human being (I had thought red-hot linotypes composed their staff) who was pleased with the tribute to his knowledge of Chaucer.

Per contra, I have had miraculous escapes in technical matters, which make me blush still. Luckily the men of the seas and the engine-room do not write to the Press, and my worst slip is still underided.

The nearest shave that ever missed me was averted by my Daemon. I was at the moment in Canada, where a young Englishman gave me, as a personal experience, a story of a body-snatching episode in deep snow, perpetrated in some lonely prairie-town and culminating in purest horror. To get it out of the system I wrote it detailedly, and it came away just a shade too good; too well-balanced; too slick. I put it aside, not that I was actively uneasy about it, but I wanted to make sure. Months passed, and I started a tooth which I took to the dentist in the little American town near 'Naulakha. ' I had to wait a while in his parlour, where I found a file of bound Harper's Magazines—say six hundred pages to the volume—dating from the 'fifties. I picked up one, and read as undistractedly as the tooth permitted. There I found my tale, identical in every mark—frozen ground, frozen corpse stiff in its fur robes in the buggy—the inn-keeper offering it a drink—and so on to the ghastly end. Had I published that tale, what could have saved me from the charge of deliberate plagiarism? Note here. Always, in our trade, look a gift horse at both ends and in the middle. He may throw you.

But here is a curious case. In the late summer, I think, of '13, I was invited to Manoeuvres round Frensham Ponds at Aldershot. The troops were from the Eighth Division of the coming year— Guardsmen, Black Watch, and the rest, down to the horsed maxims—two per battalion. Many of the officers had been juniors in the Boer War, known to Gwynne, one of the guests, and some to me. When the sham fight was developing, the day turned blue-hazy, the sky lowered, and the heat struck like the Karroo, as one scuttled among the heaths, listening to the uncontrolled clang of the musketry fire. It came over me that anything might be afoot in such weather, pom-poms for instance, half heard on a flank, or the glint of a helio through a cloud-drift. In short I conceived the whole pressure of our dead of the Boer War flickering and re-forming as the horizon flickered in the heat; the galloping feet of a single horse, and a voice once well-known that passed chanting ribaldry along the flank of a crack battalion. ('But Winnie is one of the lost—poor dear! ' was that song, if any remember it or its Singer in 1900-1901.) In an interval, while we lay on the grass, I told Gwynne what was in my head; and some officers also listened. The finale was to be manoeuvres abandoned and a hurried calling-off of all arms by badly frightened Commandants—the men themselves sweating with terror though they knew not why.

Gwynne played with the notion, and added details of Boer fighting that I did not know; and I remember a young Duke of Northumberland, since dead, who was interested. The notion so obsessed me that I wrote out the beginning at once. But in cold blood it seemed more and more fantastic and absurd, unnecessary and hysterical. Yet, three or four times I took it up and, as many, laid it down. After the War I threw the draft away. It would have done no good, and might have opened the door, and my mail, to unprofitable discussion. For there is a type of mind that dives after what it calls 'psychical experiences. ' And I am in no way 'psychic. ' Dealing as I have done with large, superficial areas of incident and occasion, one is bound to make a few lucky hits or happy deductions. But there is no need to drag in the 'clairvoyance, ' or the rest of the modern jargon. I have seen too much evil and sorrow and wreck of good minds on the road to Endor to take one step along that perilous track. Once only was I sure that I had 'passed beyond the bounds of ordinance. ' I dreamt that I stood, in my best clothes, which I do not wear as a rule, one in a line of similarly habited men, in some vast hall, floored with rough jointed stone slabs. Opposite me, the width of the hall, was another line of persons and the impression of a crowd behind them. On my left some ceremony was taking place that I wanted to see, but could not unless I stepped out of my line because the fat stomach of my neighbour on my left barred my vision. At the ceremony's close, both lines of spectators broke up and moved forward and met, and the great space filled with people. Then a man came up behind me, slipped his hand beneath my arm, and said; 'I want a word with you. ' I forget the rest; but it had been a perfectly clear dream, and it stuck in my memory. Six weeks or more later, I attended in my capacity of a Member of the War Graves Commission a ceremony at Westminster Abbey, where the Prince of Wales dedicated a plaque to 'The Million Dead' of the Great War. We Commissioners lined up facing, across the width of the Abbey Nave, more members of the Ministry and a big body of the public behind them, all in black clothes. I could see nothing of the ceremony because the stomach of the man on my left barred my vision. Then, my eye was caught by the cracks of the stone flooring, and I said to myself 'But here is where I have been! ' We broke up, both lines flowed forward and met, and the Nave filled with a crowd, through which a man came up and slipped his hand upon my arm saying; 'I want a word with you, please. ' It was about some utterly trivial matter that I have forgotten.

But how, and why, had I been shown an unreleased roll of my life-film? For the sake of the 'weaker brethren'—and sisters—I made no use of the experience.

In respect to verifying one's references, which is a matter in which one can help one's Daemon, it is curious how loath a man is to take his own medicine. Once, on a Boxing Day, with hard frost coming greasily out of the ground, my friend, Sir John Bland-Sutton, the head of the College of Surgeons, came down to 'Bateman's' very full of a lecture which he was to deliver on 'gizzards. ' We were settled before the fire after lunch, when he volunteered that So-and-so had said that if you hold a hen to your ear, you can hear the click in its gizzard of the little pebbles that help its digestion. 'Interesting, ' said I. 'He's an authority. ' 'Oh yes, but'—a long pause—'have you any hens about here, Kipling? 'I owned that I had, two hundred yards down a lane, but why not accept So-and-so? ' 'I can't, ' said John simply, 'till I've tried it. ' Remorselessly, he worried me into taking him to the hens, who lived in an open shed in front of the gardener's cottage. As we skated over the glairy ground, I saw an eye at the corner of the drawn-down Boxing-Day blind, and knew that my character for sobriety would be blasted all over the farms before night-fall. We caught an outraged pullet. John soothed her for a while (he said her pulse was a hundred and twenty-six), and held her to his ear. 'She clicks all right, ' he announced. 'Listen. ' I did, and there was click enough for a lecture. 'Now we can go back to the house, ' I pleaded. 'Wait a bit. Let's catch that cock. He'll click better. ' We caught him after a loud and long chase, and he clicked like a solitaire-board. I went home, my ears alive with parasites, so wrapped up in my own indignation that the fun of it escaped me. It had not been my verification, you see.

But John was right. Take nothing for granted if you can check it. Even though that seem waste-work, and has nothing to do with the essentials of things, it encourages the Daemon. There are always men who by trade or calling know the fact or the inference that you put forth. If you are wrong by a hair in this, they argue 'False in one thing, false in all. ' Having sinned, I know. Likewise, never play down to your public—not because some of them do not deserve it, but because it is bad for your hand. All your material is drawn from the lives of men. Remember, then, what David did with the water brought to him in the heat of battle.

And, if it be in your power, bear serenely with imitators. My Jungle Books begat Zoos of them. But the genius of all the genii was one who wrote a series called Tarzan of the Apes. I read it, but regret I never saw it on the films, where it rages most successfully. He had 'jazzed' the motif of the Jungle Books and, I imagine, had thoroughly enjoyed himself. He was reported to have said that he wanted to find out how bad a book he could write and 'get away with, ' which is a legitimate ambition.

Another case was verses of the sort that are recited. An Edinburgh taxi-driver in the War told me that they were much in vogue among the shelters and was honoured to meet me, their author. Afterwards, I found that they were running neck-and-neck with 'Gunga Din' in the military go-as-you-pleases and on the Lower Deck, and were always ascribed to my graceful hand. They were called 'The Green Eye of the Little Yellow God. ' They described an English Colonel and his daughter at Khatmandhu in Nepal where there was a military Mess; and her lover of the name of 'mad Carew' which rhymed comfortably. The refrain was more or less 'And the green-eyed yellow Idol looking down. ' It was luscious and rampant, with a touch, I thought, of the suburban Toilet-Club school favoured by the late Mr. Oscar Wilde. Yet, and this to me was the Devil of it, it carried for one reader an awesome suggestion of 'but for the Grace of God there goes Richard Baxter. ' (Refer again to the hairdresser's model which so moved Mr. Dent Pitman.) Whether the author had done it out of his own head, or as an inspired parody of the possibilities latent in a fellow-craftsman, I do not know. But I admired him.

Occasionally one could test a plagiarist. I had to invent a tree, with name to match, for a man who at that time was rather riding in my pocket. In about eighteen months—the time it takes for a 'test' diamond, thrown over the wires into a field of 'blue' rock, to turn up on the Kimberley sorting-tables—my tree appeared in his 'nature-studies' name as spelt by me and virtues attributed. Since in our trade we be all felons, more or less, I repented when I had caught him, but not too much.

And I would charge you for the sake of your daily correspondence, never to launch a glittering generality, which an older generation used to call 'Tupperism. ' Long ago I stated that 'East was East and West was West and never the twain should meet. ' It seemed right, for I had checked it by the card, but I was careful to point out circumstances under which cardinal points ceased to exist. Forty years rolled on, and for a fair half of them the excellent and uplifted of all lands would write me, apropos of each new piece of broad-minded folly in India, Egypt, or Ceylon, that East and West had met—as, in their muddled minds, I suppose they had. Being a political Calvinist, I could not argue with these condemned ones. But their letters had to be opened and filed.

Again. I wrote a song called 'Mandalay' which, tacked to a tune with a swing, made one of the waltzes of that distant age. A private soldier reviews his loves and, in the chorus, his experiences in the Burma campaign. One of his ladies lives at Moulmein, which is not on the road to anywhere, and he describes the amour with some minuteness, but always in his chorus deals with 'the road to Mandalay, ' his golden path to romance. The inhabitants of the United States, to whom I owed most of the bother, 'Panamaed' that song (this was before copyright), set it to their own tunes, and sang it in their own national voices. Not content with this, they took to pleasure cruising, and discovered that Moulmein did not command any view of any sun rising across the Bay of Bengal. They must have interfered too with the navigation of the Irrawaddy Flotilla steamers, for one of the Captains S. O.S. -ed me to give him 'something to tell these somethinged tourists about it. ' I forget what word I sent, but I hoped it might help.

Had I opened the chorus of the song with 'Oh' instead of 'On the road, ' etc., it might have shown that the song was a sort of general mix-up of the singer's Far-Eastern memories against a background of the Bay of Bengal as seen at dawn from a troop-ship taking him there. But 'On' in this case was more singable than 'Oh. ' That simple explanation may stand as a warning.

Lastly—and this got under my skin because it touched something that mattered—when, after the Boer War, there seemed an off chance of introducing conscription into England, I wrote verses called 'The Islanders' which, after a few days' newspaper correspondence, were dismissed as violent, untimely, and untrue. In them I had suggested that it was unwise to 'grudge a year of service to the lordliest life on earth. ' In the immediate next lines I described the life to which the year of service was grudged as: —

Ancient, effortless, ordered—cycle on cycle set—
Life so long untroubled that ye who inherit forget
It was not made with the mountains; it is not one with the deep.
Men, not Gods, devised it. Men, not Gods, must keep.

In a very little while it was put about that I had said that 'a year of compulsory service' would be 'effortless, ordered, ' etc. etc. —with the rider that I didn't know much about it. This perversion was perversified by a man who ought to have known better; and I suppose I should have known that it was part of the 'effortless, ordered' drift towards Armageddon. You ask; 'Why inflict on us legends of your Middle Ages? ' Because in life as in literature, its sole enduring record, is no age. Men and Things come round again, eternal as the seasons.

But, attacking or attacked, so long as you have breath, on no provocation explain. What you have said may be justified by things or some man, but never take a hand in a 'dog-fight' that opens 'My attention has been drawn to, ' etc.

I came near to breaking this Law with Punch, an institution I always respected for its continuity and its utter Englishdom, and from whose files I drew my modern working history. I had written during the Boer War a set of verses based on unofficial criticisms of many serious junior officers. (Incidentally they contained one jewel of a line that opened 'And which it may subsequently transpire'—a galaxy of words I had long panted to place in the literary firmament.) Nobody loved them, and indeed they were not conciliatory; but Punch took them rather hard. This was a pity because Punch would have been useful at that juncture. I knew none of its staff, but I asked questions and learned that Punch on this particular issue was—non-Aryan 'and German at that. ' It is true that the Children of Israel are 'people of the Book, ' and in the second Surah of the Koran Allah is made to say; 'High above mankind have I raised you. ' Yet, later, in the fifth Surah, it is written; 'Oft as they kindle a beacon-fire for war, shall God quench it. And their aim will be to abet disorder on the earth but God loveth not the abettors of disorder. ' More important still, my bearer in Lahore never announced our good little Jew tyler but he spat loudly and openly in the verandah. I swallowed my spittle at once. Israel is a race to leave alone. It abets disorder.

Many years later, during the War, The Times, with which I had had no dealings for a dozen years or so, was 'landed' with what purported to be some verses by me, headed 'The Old Volunteer. ' They had been sent in by a Sunday mail with some sort of faked postmark and without any covering letter. They were stamped with a rubber-stamp from the village office, they were written on an absolutely straight margin, which is beyond my powers, and in an un-European fist. (I had never since typewriters began sent out press-work unless it was typed.) From my point of view the contribution should not have deceived a messenger-boy. Ninthly and lastly, they were wholly unintelligible.

Human nature being what it is, The Times was much more annoyed with me than anyone else, though goodness knows—this, remember, was in '17—I did not worry them about it, beyond hinting that the usual week-end English slackness, when no one is in charge, had made the mess. They took the matter up with the pomp of the Public Institution which they were, and submitted the MS. to experts, who proved that it must be the work of a man who had all but 'spoofed' The Times about some fragments of Keats. He happened to be an old friend of mine, and when I told him of his magnified 'characteristic' letters, and the betraying slopes at which they lay—his, as I pointed out, 'very C's and U's and T's, ' he was wrath and, being a poet, swore a good deal that if he could not have done a better parody of my 'stuff' with his left hand he would retire from business. This I believed, for, on the heels of my modest disclaimer which appeared, none too conspicuously, in The Times, I had had a letter in a chaffing vein about 'The Old Volunteer' from a non-Aryan who never much appreciated me; and the handwriting of it, coupled with the subtlety of choosing a week-end (as the Hun had chosen August Bank Holiday of '14) for the work, plus the Oriental detachedness and insensitiveness of playing that sort of game in the heart of a life-and-death struggle, made me suspect him more than a little. He is now in Abraham's bosom, so I shall never know. But The Times seemed very happy with its enlarged letters, and measurements of the alphabet, and—there really was a war on which filled my days and nights. Then The Times sent down a detective to my home. I didn't see the drift of this, but naturally was interested. And It was a Detective out of a book, down to the very creaks of Its boots. (On the human side at lunch It knew a lot about second-hand furniture.) Officially, It behaved like all the detectives in the literature of that period. Finally, It settled Itself, back to the light, facing me at my work-table, and told me a long yarn about a man who worried the Police with complaints of anonymous letters addressed to him from unknown sources, all of which, through the perspicacity of the Police, turned out to have been written by himself to himself for the purpose of attracting notoriety. As in the case of the young man on the Canadian train, that tale felt as though it had come out of a magazine of the 'sixties; and I was so interested in its laborious evolution that I missed its implication till quite the end. Then I got to thinking of the psychology of the detective, and what a gay life of plots It must tramp through; and of the psychology of The Times-in-a-hole, which is where no one shows to advantage; and of how Moberly Bell, whose bows I had crossed in the old days, would have tackled the matter; what Buckle, whom I loved for his sincerity and gentlehood, would have thought of it all. Thus I forgot to defend my 'injured honour. ' The thing had passed out of reason into the Higher Hysterics. What could I do but offer It some more sherry and thank It for a pleasant interview?

I have told this at length because Institutions of idealistic tendencies sometimes wait till a man is dead, and then furnish their own evidence. Should this happen, try to believe that in the deepest trough of the War I did not step aside to play with The Times, Printing House Square, London, E.C.

In the come-and-go of family talk there was often discussion as to whether I could write a 'real novel. ' The Father thought that the setting of my work and life would be against it, and Time justified him.

Now here is a curious thing. At the Paris Exhibition of 1878 I saw, and never forgot, a picture of the death of Marion Lescaut, and asked my Father many questions. I read that amazing 'one book' of the Abbé Prévost, in alternate slabs with Scarron's Roman Comique, when I was about eighteen, and it brought up the picture. My theory is that a germ lay dormant till my change of life to London (though that is not Paris) woke it up, and that The Light that Failed was a sort of inverted, metagrobolised phantasmagoria based on Manon. I was confirmed in my belief when the French took to that conte with relish, and I always fancied that it walked better in translation than in the original. But it was only a conte—not a built book.

Kim, of course, was nakedly picaresque and plotless—a thing imposed from without.

Yet I dreamed for many years of building a veritable three-decker out of chosen and longstored timber-teak, green-heart, and ten-year-old oak knees—each curve melting deliciously into the next that the sea might nowhere meet resistance or weakness; the whole suggesting motion even when, her great sails for the moment furled, she lay in some needed haven—a vessel ballasted on ingots of pure research and knowledge, roomy, fitted with delicate cabinet-work below-decks, painted, carved, gilt and wreathed the length of her, from her blazing stern-galleries outlined by bronzy palm-trunks, to her rampant figure-head—an East Indiaman worthy to lie alongside The Cloister and the Hearth.

Not being able to do this, I dismissed the ambition as 'beneath the thinking mind.' So does a half-blind man dismiss shooting and golf.

Nor did I live to see the day when the new three-deckers should hoist themselves over the horizon, quivering to their own power, over-loaded with bars, ball-rooms, and insistent chromium plumbing; hellishly noisy from the sports' deck to the barber's shop; but serving their generation as the old craft served theirs. The young men were already laying down the lines of them, fondly believing that the old laws of design and construction were for them abrogated.

And with what tools did I work in my own mould-loft? I had always been choice, not to say coquettish in this respect. In Lahore for my Plain Tales I used a slim, octagonal-sided, agate penholder with a Waverley nib. It was a gift, and when in an evil hour it snapped I was much disturbed. Then followed a procession of impersonal hirelings each with a Waverley, and next a silver penholder with a quill-like curve, which promised well but did not perform. In Villiers Street I got me an outsize office pewter ink-pot, on which I would gouge the names of the tales and books I wrote out of it. But the housemaids of married life polished those titles away till they grew as faded as a palimpsest.

I then abandoned hand-dipped Waverleys—a nib I never changed—and for years wallowed in the pin-pointed 'stylo' and its successor the 'fountain' which for me meant geyser-pens. In later years I clung to a slim, smooth, black treasure (Jael was her office name) which I picked up in Jerusalem. I tried pump-pens with glass insides, but they were of 'intolerable entrails. '

For my ink I demanded the blackest, and had I been in my Father's house, as once I was, would have kept an ink-boy to grind me Indian-ink. All 'blue-blacks' were an abomination to my Daemon, and I never found a bottled vermilion fit to rubricate initials when one hung in the wind waiting.

My writing-blocks were built for me to an unchanged pattern of large, off-white, blue sheets, of which I was most wasteful. All this old-maiderie did not prevent me when abroad from buying and using blocks, and tackle, in any country.

With a lead pencil I ceased to express—probably because I had to use a pencil in reporting. I took very few notes except of names, dates, and addresses. If a thing didn't stay in my memory, I argued it was hardly worth writing out. But each man has his own method. I rudely drew what I wanted to remember.

Like most men who ply one trade in one place for any while, I always kept certain gadgets on my work-table, which was ten feet long from North to South and badly congested. One was a long, lacquer, canoe-shaped pen-tray full of brushes and dead 'fountains'; a wooden box held clips and bands; another, a tin one, pins; yet another, a bottle-slider, kept all manner of unneeded essentials from emery-paper to small screwdrivers; a paper-weight, said to have been Warren Hastings' a tiny, weighted fur-seal and a leather crocodile sat on some of the papers; an inky foot-rule and a Father of Penwipers which a much-loved housemaid of ours presented yearly, made up the main-guard of these little fetishes.

My treatment of books, which I looked upon as tools of my trade, was popularly regarded as barbarian. Yet I economised on my multitudinous penknives, and it did no harm to my fore-finger. There were books which I respected, because they were put in locked cases. The others, all the house over, took their chances.

Left and right of the table were two big globes, on one of which a great airman had once outlined in white paint those air-routes to the East and Australia which were well in use before my death.